D1376490

IT COULD

HAPPEN

HERE

A Novel

It Could Happen Here

Greg Watson

ISBN: 978-1-73247-045-3

© 2018. All rights reserved. No part of this publication may be reproduced, distributed, or transmitted in any form or by any means, including photocopying, recording, or other electronic or mechanical methods, without the prior written permission of the publisher, except in the case of brief quotations embodied in critical reviews and certain other noncommercial uses permitted by copyright law.

PROLOGUE

Eian sat at his desk at the Proteus facility in Middleville, Texas. Proteus was the world leader in internet search, social media, web email, and video hosting. Eian had been excited to work for the company. Now he wasn't so sure. He needed to make an edit to the company's algorithm, something for which he had little experience as a non-programmer. Yet he plunged ahead. He made the edit, and then he hit reload on the screen which would show the update live to the world. He had made a syntax edit error. The raw code would be exposed momentarily to anyone now on the Internet. Eian quickly fixed the syntax error, and then hit reload. All was good. Hopefully, no one noticed the mistake.

Across town, Alex sat at his laptop, getting ready for a camping trip. As he prepared to shut down his computer, he noticed something odd on the Proteus search page. There he saw the name of Brother Davis, pastor of First Baptist of Middleville, hard-coded into raw computer code. He quickly attempted to make a screenshot. Before he could, however, the code was gone. The main Proteus search page appeared as usual.

Alex sat wondering. Why would Proteus have Brother Davis's name hard-coded into its code? His mind raced for an explanation.

Perhaps he hadn't seen it? But he had. As he sat wondering, his dad called out, "Alex, you'd better get going. It's getting late."

Alex packed the last of his things into the back of the truck. He wanted to get to the other side of the lake and set up camp before nightfall. He had just enough time. Alex snapped his fingers and pointed to the back of the truck for his dog—a Doberman—to jump in.

"Come on, Rex. In you go, boy."

"So, you want to camp out over there all night again?" Alex's father, Drew, asked.

"Come on, Dad. It isn't like I haven't done anything like this before. And besides, I've got my bodyguard," Alex said as he pointed to Rex in back of the truck. His father smiled. But he still didn't want him to go.

Alex was the younger of two children in the family. Allison was away at college at Texas Heritage. Their mother had died tragically in a plane crash when Alex was just 12. Although four years had passed, his father was still dealing with the painful loss of his wife. To help comfort himself, Drew doted on his children and struggled against overprotecting them. At the same time, however, Drew wanted to encourage them to live life, and fully explore whatever interested them.

Alex's interests were wide-ranging, everything from comics to computers to archery. Alex's interests included photography, especially nighttime photography of owls. It was something that felt strange to share with someone who hadn't experienced it. Getting a night shot of an owl after patiently waiting and managing to hold the camera at just the right angle was extremely challenging, yet thrilling when you saw the photo you worked so hard to get.

Along with photography, Alex also enjoyed archery. To prevent his son from wildly sending arrows into a neighbor's backyard, Drew had an archery cage-like structure built in the backyard. Inside the cage, Alex could safely be off target with no harm to anyone.

Alex liked the idea of having his bow and arrows with him when camping. He couldn't imagine using the bow in the woods. Having it with him, though, along with having Rex, gave him an added feeling of security when camping alone.

Drew helped Alex pack his camera equipment, tent gear, supplies, and his bow and arrows in the truck. They wouldn't see each other for nearly a week. Drew was a pilot with World Express. It was a job that offered him a lot of flexibility and time at home, but it also meant leaving Alex by himself. Drew felt safe enough leaving Alex alone, though, especially with Rex.

"Be careful over there, son. I'm flying out tonight. I'll give you a call in the morning," Drew said.

"Have a good trip, Dad. And don't worry, I'll be fine," replied Alex.

Alex headed down the driveway to the road which circled Lake Vista. The lake was the development brainchild of the town's favored son—business tycoon Sam Jones—who maintained a home on the lake. Lake Vista had been Sam Jones's first significant investment in his hometown of Middleville, Texas. He worked with a team—developers, environmentalists, and others—to plan the design of the lake. One side was a gated community of large, high-end homes at different price ranges. The other side consisted of a large, wooded preserve interwoven with nature trails and camping areas, which were open to the public. At the far end of this side of the lake were a small beach and picnic area with a rock climbing wall built into one side.

It was about half an hour before sunset as Alex turned into the campground parking area. As he shut off the engine, he stopped for a moment to look into the woods. When he first attempted to camp out all night in the woods alone, he lost his nerve and had to head back home. Gradually, though, he had come to enjoy and even look forward to the nighttime solitude.

"Wanna give me hand, boy?" Alex said to Rex as he gathered his camera gear, camping supplies, and bow from the back of the truck. He could just manage to carry everything in one trip. Alex talked freely with his dog as if Rex understood his every word.

He reached his campsite in the middle of the woods. From this location, he could see the clearing at the far side of the woods, sloping down to the beach picnic area near the water. Alex took out his night vision binoculars and scanned the trees. No sign yet of any night owls. He then set up his camera equipment, took out some beef jerky and threw a few strips to Rex. "Good stuff, buddy," he said, as he rubbed his dog's head.

He decided to set up camp for the night. He turned on his night lantern, took his tent out, set it up, and unfolded the sleeping bag inside. He carefully, and this time slowly, scanned the trees above. He spotted an owl. Holding the night vision binoculars steady with one hand, he moved toward the camera mounted on a tripod, careful not to lose sight of the owl as he switched from binoculars to the camera.

He focused the camera and took the shot. "Got one, Rex," he said, as he couldn't help but share the good news. Rex stared back at Alex then licked his hand, perhaps searching for more beef jerky.

Alex decided to go into his tent for the night. His father had found him a tent especially designed for camping with Rex. There was a main compartment for Alex, and attached to this was a kind of side-car compartment for Rex. Inside the tent, Alex looked through the pictures he had taken and transferred some to his phone. He then read through a couple of comic books, talked with Rex a little, and started to doze off.

He was roused out of his drowsiness by the faint sound of voices at the far end of the camping area. Rex heard the voices too and was now sitting upright. Alex hadn't remembered seeing any other cars when he pulled in earlier. There was a parking lot on the other side of the rock climbing wall. But that area closed at night.

At first, Alex tried to ignore the noise, but it seemed to grow louder. He couldn't tune it out or put it out of his mind. With a mixture of curiosity, fear, and irritation he decided to investigate the source of the noise that had invaded his solitude. He grabbed his backpack and (without knowing quite why) he also grabbed his bow and arrows. With his night vision goggles around his neck, he ambled with Rex toward the rock climbing wall area.

Alex felt Rex surging forward. "Easy, buddy. It's okay," he said in an attempt to slow Rex's progress and calm his nerves.

It didn't help. Rex continued to surge forward faster than he would like, and Alex felt himself becoming more nervous than he would like. Alex paused to look through his night vision goggles.

He could now clearly see the glow of a campfire in the beach area reflected against the night.

It was then that he heard what sounded like a scream, and then a distinctly female voice saying, "No! Stop it already!"

The screams grew louder and male laughter now accompanied them. Alex quickly covered the rest of the distance to the beach and rock climbing wall area. Faster he moved. Faster Rex moved. More screams. More laughter. As Alex reached the edge of the woods, he stopped to catch his breath and motioned Rex to a halt. Hiding with Rex at his side at the top of a small hill, Alex looked down through his goggles to see what he feared he might see.

Through his goggles, Alex saw four of his high school class-mates—Jeff Taylor, Tad Smith, Matt Nelson, and Heather Swanson. The screams Alex had heard were from Heather. Jeff was stand-ing with his legs spread apart and rocking Heather back and forth between his legs. Her head was just missing the ground with each pass, which appeared to be a game of sorts on their part.

Alex was irritated with himself for becoming alarmed at the screams and laughter and annoyed with his classmates for intruding on his solitude. Alex knew Heather and all three of the guys, but they weren't friends. The guys were all football players at Middleville High School, and all three were active in the community's nation-ally known, anti-bullying program. In fact, Alex saw that Jeff was wearing a sweatshirt emblazoned with the program's rallying cry, #ProLifeNotJustProBirth. As part of the program, Alex had used his coding skills to develop a social media monitoring program. Local police, school and community leaders had all come to depend on the program, but students like Jeff and his friends resented Alex for the software's intrusion on their social lives.

Alex was getting ready to head back to his tent with Rex, but decided to take one last look through his goggles. He now noticed another person sitting off to the side at the base of the rock wall— Becky Worthington. "What's she doing here?" Alex mumbled to himself.

Alex had seen Heather with Jeff and the other football players at school, at church, and around town. Becky was new to the area, and Alex had chatted with her briefly at church and school. While Alex couldn't describe the exact type of girl who would pal around with Heather and the football players, he guessed that Becky would not be the type. There she was, though; sitting off by herself.

Alex noticed Heather appeared to be growing tired and walked away from Jeff and the guys toward the steps heading back to the parking lot behind the rock wall. She wanted to wait in her car. She paused and appeared to say something and then motioned to Becky to go back with her. Good, Alex thought. Maybe the guys will leave now too.

Instead of leaving, Jeff grabbed at Heather's sweatshirt while appearing apologetic. Heather twisted away from him and then motioned again toward Becky to accompany her back to the car.

Becky stood up and moved towards Heather. Jeff immediately walked forward in Becky's direction and blocked her way to the stairs while yelling at Heather to leave. Heather appeared torn and started yelling back. Even from atop the hill, Alex could hear part of the exchange.

"Jeff, she doesn't want to!" pleaded Heather.

"Well, unless you want some too!" Jeff yelled back.

Alex began to get nervous. What is it that Becky doesn't want to do, he wondered.

While restraining Becky, Jeff motioned to Tad in Heather's direction. Tad obeyed and started to escort Heather back to the car, but she shook her head in disgust and headed back on her own. Tad followed her up the stairs.

In what seemed like moments to Alex, Tad was heading back down the stairs, pausing to give Jeff a thumbs-up. Becky started to walk toward Tad, but Jeff grabbed her arm and pulled her back. She started to walk in the opposite direction, toward the corner where she had been sitting, but Jeff quickly blocked that way. He then grabbed her by the shoulders and pushed her up against the rock climbing wall. She tried to slap him, but he easily blocked the blow.

Rex had been lying flat at Alex's command, but he was now on all fours. Alex knew he had to do something. But could he challenge all three of them, even with Rex? He didn't know, but he would have to try. Searching quickly in his backpack, he located a can of lighter fluid he had planned to use to build a fire in the morning. He found a rag in his bag and tied it to the front end of an arrow. He then doused the rag with the lighter fluid. He readied the arrow in the bow.

Meanwhile, Becky was squirming to get away from Jeff, and she almost succeeded. Jeff motioned to Tad for help in holding her against the wall. Jeff then looked over his shoulder in Matt's direction and gave a signal of some sort. Alex looked through his goggles to get a better look. He saw Matt positioning his phone camera on the table to Jeff's left and pointing right at Jeff, Becky, and Tad.

Alex was in disbelief. He had heard stories about the off-the-field exploits of the football players, and he suspected they were something less than the role models they were made out to be in church and school. But would they do this? And film it? He hoped to wake up soon in his tent realizing the whole thing had been a bad dream.

Becky really began to put up a fight now and started kicking Jeff and Tad as they both struggled to hold her against the wall. Jeff looked over his shoulder and signaled for Matt to help him. It was now Matt, Jeff, and Tad all restraining Becky. With Matt holding her left arm and leg against the wall and Tad holding the other, Jeff released her.

Jeff took a step back and turned in the direction of the phone and smiled. He took his sweatshirt off and threw it near the fire. He then unbuttoned his jeans and stripped down to his briefs. He stepped towards Becky and reached to unbutton her jeans. She let out the loudest scream Alex had ever heard in his life. Tad tried to put his hand over her mouth. Alex knew he had to do something—and now. He looked down at Rex and said, "Get ready to move, buddy!"

He took a few steps downhill towards the fire. He aimed his arrow directly at the fire and let it fly. Bull's-eye! The flames erupted, and Jeff's sweatshirt on the ground caught fire. Jeff turned in the direction of the fire and pulled his jeans back on as he ran to grab his sweatshirt. Matt and Tad released their hold on Becky, and she broke free and ran to the corner to a picnic table and crawled under it.

Jeff had never turned Rex loose on anyone. He didn't know how he would react, but he had no choice. Pointing at Jeff, Matt, and Tad, he turned to Rex and said: "Go!"

Instead of running toward the three boys, Rex ran straight for Becky hiding under the table. Alex reloaded his bow and quickly advanced down the hill after Rex. It was Rex who reached Becky first. He came right up to where she was hiding under the table. Alex could see her eyes widen. Upon reaching her, Rex turned away from her in the direction of Jeff, Matt, and Tad. His bared his teeth and all of his neck muscles arched. He was in full combat mode.

As he walked quickly toward Rex, Alex turned and aimed his bow at Jeff who threw his hands in the air and walked toward the steps back to the parking lot. Tad and Matt were already at the bottom of stairs. Before leaving, Jeff turned towards Alex and yelled, "Have a good time, Alex."

Alex watched the three go up the stairs while he still had the bow pointed at them. Only after he could no longer see them did he release his grip on the bow. He was almost shaking with anger and fear. Alex then turned to Becky who was crying under the table. "Come on, Becky. Let's get you out of here."

As Alex crouched down to give Becky a hand in getting out from under the table, a light caught the corner of his eye. He looked to his left. Matt had left his cell phone. It had recorded everything.

ONE YEAR EARLIER

CHAPTER 1

Sam Jones finished putting a pan of biscuits in the oven and walked into the sunroom to call Mr. Simmons, who was his business mentor and close friend. Mr. Simmons was one of the few people able to call Sam Jones "Sam," and despite knowing each other for decades, Sam Jones wouldn't think of calling Mr. Simmons anything other than "Mr. Simmons."

"Hello there, Mr. Simmons. I do believe I've outdone myself with this pan of biscuits. You'd better get over here and have some with me."

"I'm sure they'll be great, Sam. Be right over."

As he hung up the phone to prepare to make the short drive over to Sam Jones's house, Mr. Simmons chuckled at the thought of Sam Jones—the billionaire—still enjoying making biscuits.

Mr. Simmons pulled his Lincoln out of the driveway and headed toward Jones's house. Although Mr. Simmons's house was quite large, it was dwarfed by Jones's—the largest house on Lake Vista. It consisted of ten bedrooms, eight bathrooms, a library, a huge game room, a massive outdoor kitchen, and an even larger indoor kitchen. The view of the lake from the house's sunroom offered a picturesque view. *Architectural Monthly* had profiled the house with the feature article predictably titled "Keeping Up with the Joneses."

Jones's house was large enough to house a live-in cook, Joan; a maid, Maria; and Jones's assistant, Jonathan. There was also ample room for Jones's son, Tyler, and daughter, Nicole, and their families to visit. In addition to his palatial home in Middleville, Jones also owned large apartments in Houston and New York, and these were large enough for his staff and family to stay with him.

Jones's treatment of his employees, especially his personal staff, was atypical for a man of his vast means. He went the extra mile and then some to be generous and fair. He paid his employees well. And despite having a volcanic temper if left unchecked, Jones made a point of keeping his cool in dealing with subordinates, especially those of lesser rank. He was most generous to his personal staff, financing boarding school and college for the children of his maid, cook, and personal assistant. After graduation, Jones assisted them in finding a place within his organization or "anywhere they wanted to go" within their chosen field.

The extravagance Jones displayed didn't bother Mr. Simmons in the least. Mr. Simmons thought Jones had come by his wealth honestly and in his generosity to his employees, to Middleville, and to a variety of charities, Jones embodied the big spending Texan in a way Mr. Simmons could look to with admiration and pride.

Mr. Simmons was proud of the national notoriety Jones brought to Middleville, and he was proud of the part that he had played in Jones's success. Jones had proven his investment savvy many times over. Yet he still sought the advice of Mr. Simmons, who was only too happy to give it.

Mr. Simmons, long the town's elder statesman, had helped shepherd Middleville through uncertain economic times, as the city transitioned from one centered around a military base to a varied commercial community. Jones was a student at Texas Heritage in the late 1970s when Mr. Simmons began to guide Middleville through this economic transition.

Jones had every reason not to return home to Middleville after graduation. Yet he could see opportunity where others could not. He agreed with Mr. Simmons: The former military base occupied or was adjacent to some of the best real estate in town. All it needed was a visionary to develop it. Jones was that visionary. Fresh out of college and newly married to his college girlfriend, Linda, Jones returned to Middleville, where with the initial backing of Mr. Simmons he would put Middleville on the road to prosperity and build one of the largest investment and commercial real estate firms in the world.

The Simmons family was one of the oldest and wealthiest in Middleville. In town, there was Simmons Furniture, Simmons Ford, Simmons Hardware, and The Middleville Daily, all inherited and owned by Mr. Simmons. Even with his wealth, Mr. Simmons knew that with the loss of the town's military base, it would take more investment if Middleville were to have a future. Taking a portion of his fortune, he set up an investment fund to be used to attract businesses to Middleville. Mr. Simmons asked Sam Jones to help him manage the fund. Seeing how well he understood the markets, Mr. Simmons turned over the management of a portion of his investments to Jones. As he continued to exceed expectations, Mr. Simmons helped him establish Jones Investments, which would eventually become the global behemoth, Jones Enterprises.

Much of Jones's success stemmed from his ability to invest in or cash out of the market at critical points, sometimes in a direction contrary to prevailing opinion. His first big break came shortly before the stock market crash in 1987 when, sensing instability in the market, Jones cashed out most of his clients' funds. He invested early in technology stocks in the early 1990s but managed to sell off before the demise of many internet-related companies. By steering clear of mortgage-related investments, Jones managed to emerge from the 2008 financial crisis relatively unscathed.

As Jones became a wealthy man, he gave generously to Middleville. More than giving money, however, Jones thought it important to invest in the overall health of the community. Hence, he was a big supporter of local leaders in law enforcement and schools. And although an infrequent church attendee, Jones was an enthusiastic supporter of local churches and their outreach ministries to the local community.

One program in particular which interested Jones was the anti-bullying initiative, dubbed by First Baptist's Youth Pastor Crabtree as the #ProLifeNotJustProBirth movement. It was started and led by Pastor Jack Davis or "Brother Davis," as he was known to his congregation at First Baptist Church of Middleville. Brother Davis's program commanded Jones's support based on the experience of his family in Jones's teen years in Middleville.

Jones grew up moving every few years as his father changed assignments in the Air Force. When he was a sophomore in high school, his father took an overseas assignment, but in his absence decided to relocate the family to Middleville, where Jones could finish high school and his sister, Kate, could finish middle school.

With each move the family made, Jones found it easy to fit in and adapt. He excelled academically, socially, and he played sports. By contrast, Kate was socially awkward, and some of her classmates cruelly taunted her; however, she mostly kept this from her mother and brother.

In high school, Kate began experimenting with drugs. She began her first stint in rehab at age 19. Jones blamed himself for not being more aware of his sister's plight in school. He felt he had let his family down and tried to make amends by doing everything to make Kate's adult life in Middleville as pleasant as possible. He helped her open a beauty salon downtown and helped her attract customers.

Preventing what happened to his sister in school from happening to someone else was what attracted Jones to Brother Davis's anti-bullying program. He liked that the program involved students, parents, clergy, and school and law enforcement officials. He used his influence in town to encourage the program and was its most generous financial supporter. Jones was especially proud that the program had achieved notoriety beyond Middleville as a model of its kind.

Jones was putting a pot of coffee on the table in the sunroom as Mr. Simmons pulled into the driveway. Mr. Simmons had a key to the house, but he rarely used it unless Jones wasn't home. Jones had given Joan and Maria the morning off, and his wife was a late sleeper. But he was only too happy to assume the kitchen duties for his good friend, Mr. Simmons.

"Smells good, Sam," Mr. Simmons said as he walked into the kitchen.

"Well, good morning to you, Mr. Simmons. Just made some coffee, and the biscuits should be ready here in a minute."

Jones then launched into a lengthy discussion with Mr. Simmons about various investments. He valued Mr. Simmons's investment advice. He had long discovered Mr. Simmons enjoyed such a lengthy discussion, even if they both could quickly determine the best course of action.

The discussion moved on to the topic of The Texas Tornadoes— the pro football team Jones had owned for eight years. Despite his success in business, Jones had not been able to produce a winning football team. He looked forward, however, to the opening of a massive, new domed stadium for the team, which was scheduled for completion next year.

"How do your Tornadoes look for next year?" Mr. Simmons asked.

"I tell you the truth. I seem to have a proven formula for mediocrity, Mr. Simmons. I hope a change of scenery might help things, though. Say that reminds me. I'm going next Monday to get a tour of how things are progressing on the new stadium. How about if you come along with me?"

"Sure. I'd enjoy that," Mr. Simmons replied.

Jones had been busy planning every detail for the grand opening of the stadium. He eagerly shared some of these details with Mr. Simmons.

"I've been going over plans with Jonathan for opening night in the new stadium. He has sold me on the idea of a Texas High School All-Star Game. And the more I think about it, the more I like the idea. It will give us a chance to show off our boys, as much for the kind of young men they are as for the way they play football."

"That reminds me, Sam," added Mr. Simmons, as he shifted uneasily in his chair.

"About the boys—well, I had an encounter with a few of them last month at the drug store," Mr. Simmons said.

"What happened?" Jones asked.

Mr. Simmons went on to describe the encounter in the drug store. Although it had been over a month, he could still remember everything well.

"As I was heading towards the register, one of the young men came down the aisle toward me and just as he pulled even with me, he lowered his shoulder, knocking me into the shelf and nearly to the ground."

Jones knew Mr. Simmons liked to enjoy an occasional elaborate joke. He smiled politely in anticipation of the punch line.

"And then what happened?" Jones added, still holding a smile.

"I reached down on the floor in the aisle to pick up a few items that he knocked out of the basket when he ran into me. When I did, I couldn't help but notice another young fella at the end of the aisle. As I looked his way, he smiled and snapped my picture with his cell phone and ran off."

Uncharacteristically for Mr. Simmons, Jones couldn't quite discern the direction of the story. But he had a momentary thought: Could Mr. Simmons be serious?

"Well, you had me going there, Mr. Simmons," said Jones with an obligatory laugh.

"Sam, I wish this were only a story I made up for a laugh."

The smile fell from Jones's face. He nearly dropped his coffee mug. He stared at Mr. Simmons.

"You mean to tell me this really happened to you?"

Mr. Simmons nodded in agreement. Jones pounded the table. Stood up. Swore mightily. And then quickly apologized. Mr. Simmons chuckled.

"I'm all right, Sam. I am concerned, though, about our boys. I wonder if we're all building them up to be something that they're not."

Jones raised his eyebrows and nodded slowly in agreement. He then collected his thoughts. That someone (especially a young person) could knock over someone (especially an older person) in public, seemingly for entertainment, was something utterly alien to him. It violated every code of ethics and civility he had ever known.

"Who were the boys who did this?" Jones asked.

"Well, I don't want to get anyone in trouble," Mr. Simmons replied.

"They won't be this time. But this has to be dealt with. Now I know you don't want to get anyone in trouble, and I don't either, but who were these boys?"

"It was Jeff Taylor and the Smith boy. Tad Smith, I believe it is. I'm not sure I would have recognized them, except for the fact that their faces are on the billboard as you come into town."

Jones thought for a moment about the billboard and immediately knew who the boys were. Although he only occasionally drove into town (preferring to fly in, instead), he had remarked on the billboard, and he took a certain amount of pride in what it represented. The billboard featured a row of young people in different colored tee shirts. The two athletes, Jeff and Tad, were flanked by two girls on each side, both cheerleaders. Underneath the picture of the young people were the words, "Middleville: Where Nice People Rule."

Mr. Simmons left a short time later. But Jones continued to consider what he had learned. Something had gone wrong. The image of the character of the town's young people he had built up in his mind did not correspond to reality. What had gone wrong?

Later that day Jones called Bill Weston—the town's chief of police—and also called Brother Davis. Both could not have been more understanding and apologetic, and they both promised to talk with the boys, but something about the way they both reacted bothered Jones. Rather than being as shocked as he was by the news, they both responded as if they both either knew about the incident or didn't see it as wildly out of character for the boys. Were the actions of the boys now the accepted norm? Furthermore, how did Chief Weston and especially Brother Davis reconcile the behavior of the boys with the popular image of their characters that they both promoted? He didn't have the answers to these questions, but he intended to find out.

CHAPTER 2

Brother Davis was sitting at his desk in his office at First Baptist of Middleville when h is phone buzzed. It was his secretary, Gail McBride, reminding him of his next appointment in half an hour. Davis thanked her and then proceeded with his reading.

Since his college days at Texas Temple, Davis had made it a point to be an avid reader, not only of books typically read by pastors—such as commentaries and sermon collections—but also history, classic literature, and philosophy. He also made it a point to stay on a reading schedule. And he was at this point bringing up the calculator on the computer in his office and calculating the number of pages per week he should read of Plato's *Republic* to finish it by the end of the year. In the middle of performing these calculations, he grew frustrated and abandoned the effort. Although he did read widely, he set overly ambitious goals for himself and became frustrated when he invariably failed to meet them.

With fifteen minutes remaining before his next appointment, Davis turned his attention to the new member application before him. He noticed that Eian Braymore, the gentleman soon to arrive, had been baptized at Plainsville Baptist Church in Plainsville, Indiana. This news delighted Davis. Bill Cook, the pastor at Plainsville

Baptist, had been his classmate at Texas Temple, and he even now occasionally exchanged emails with him. Davis stopped reading over the application, and (and as he often did) mentally relived moments of his past.

It had been his father's idea to send him to Texas Temple in the late 1970s. Davis grew up in suburban Houston in Flint, Texas, where his father owned a construction business and also served as a deacon at First Baptist Church of Flint. Davis's father was an avid reader of Baptist books and periodicals. Some of what he read concerned him. Fearing the Southern Baptist Convention was heading the way of mainline liberalism, he felt safer sending his son to an Independent Baptist school like Texas Temple. Since many of his friends were attending Southern Baptist-affiliated Maylor University, Davis was at first less than enamored with his father's choice. But his respect and love for his father overrode his reluctance.

By contrast, the parents of Davis's wife, Ann, sent her to Texas Temple with some reluctance. It was not their first choice for their daughter or even in their top ten, but it was what their daughter wanted, so they consented. Ann's mother and father both worked for the evangelical publishing house, Heaton Press, affiliated with Heaton College north of Chicago. Ann's family enjoyed their life in Heaton and were active members at First Baptist Church of Heaton.

They had expected their daughter, like most of her extended family friends, to attend college at Heaton. That changed, however, when Ann was invited by a high school classmate to a revival meeting at a small, Independent Baptist church. A traveling singing group affiliated with Texas Temple was featured that night at the revival. Ann could not have enjoyed the service or the music more. It was quite informal and so unlike the style of service that she had grown up with at First Baptist. Ann met with members of the singing group after the service, and they shared information with her about Texas Temple. After praying and giving it some thought, she decided that was where she would attend college. Her parents were at first aghast, not wanting their daughter rubbing shoulders with the fundamentalist rabble. Yet Ann stuck to her decision, so they gave her their blessing.

Davis could still remember the first time he saw Ann. He had just said goodbye to his father on the chapel steps and was heading into the chapel to join the other freshman students for orientation. Ann was standing at the top of the steps talking with a couple of other students. She glanced his way, and he forgot where he was. Davis quickly asked Ann out on an on-campus date. It was the only kind permitted for freshmen at Texas Temple. From their first date, they were inseparable on campus. They ate meals together and attended required church and chapel services together, and eventually enjoyed off-campus dating, a privilege granted only to upperclassmen.

Ann was an English major and planned to join her family in the publishing business after graduation. Davis entered college unsure of his major, but gradually felt called to enter the ministry, so he became a Pastoral Studies major. His father and Ann were both supportive of him in this decision.

Studying came easier to Ann than to Davis. But he did have an intellectual curiosity and a strong work ethic. Ann also encouraged him to read widely, and with her encouragement, he began to read classic literature, and gradually began to think of himself as well read. This overconfidence would occasionally land him in embarrassing situations. One such incident occurred when he accompanied Ann home for a visit on a Thanksgiving break. Regrettably, he pronounced "Yeats" as "Yeets," and Ann's mother corrected him. Incidents like these reminded him that for all his striving, he remained (in one of his favorite phrases from Victor Hugo), "something less than a man of the world and something more."

In their final year at Temple, Ann and Davis were engaged and made plans for their life together following graduation. They planned to live with Ann's parents in suburban Chicago while Davis attended graduate school and Ann pursued an internship as an editor. Ann's internship at Heaton Press was essentially in place, and although Davis had yet to receive an acceptance letter from Heaton Graduate School, he had no doubt of his eventual acceptance.

Davis was taken aback when nearing both graduation and his marriage to Ann; he received a curtly worded rejection letter from Heaton. The letter matter-of-factly informed him that since Temple was an unaccredited institution, Heaton would be unable to recognize his degree. Davis knew Temple was unaccredited, but he also knew that despite this, some students had been accepted to secular graduate schools and many students had gone on to seminary. Ann's parents offered to intervene with the admissions staff at Heaton on his behalf, but Davis refused the help. He wanted to be accepted like any other student, or not attend at all.

With Ann's encouragement, Davis did accept other forms of assistance from her parents. They helped to obtain an internship for him at First Baptist of Heaton. They also arranged for him to be privately taught and mentored by a retired Baptist minister in the area.

This mentorship from Pastor Jim Mitchell would prove to be pivotal for the early years of Davis's ministry in Middleville.

Mitchell urged Davis to strive to find the right balance between pastoral study and visitation, telling him that to be effective as a preacher, he needed to prepare. Yet he couldn't neglect the visitation side of the ministry. Some of this could be delegated to staff and lay volunteers, but the pastor needed to be seen taking an active part. And rightly or wrongly, the congregation would expect this.

With theological conservatives becoming the dominant force in the Southern Baptist Convention, Davis's father offered to send his son to seminary at Maylor University, and pay all of his and Ann's living expenses. He and Ann at first declined the offer but eventually consented. They both knew how important having seminary training would be for anyone wanting to make the ministry his life's vocation.

Ann and Davis enjoyed their time at Maylor. Davis did well in his seminary studies and was well regarded by his classmates and professors. As comfortable as things seemed, however, on the surface, Davis occasionally felt slighted by his classmates. He was one of a handful of students with an undergraduate degree from an Independent Baptist school. In conversations with his classmates about his background, he often encountered an awkward silence when his undergraduate background became the topic of discussion. Or, he would happen to overhear a classmate telling a joke about Baptist fundamentalists, which Davis would have found funny if his classmate had not ended the fun by telling him that he "intended him no offense."

As Davis approached graduation, it so happened that First Baptist of Middleville was in need of a new pastor. After much discussion in committee, it was decided the church preferred a pastor just finishing seminary. As head of the pulpit committee, Mr. Simmons made the unusual choice to travel to Maylor to interview candidates first-hand.

A special room was set up on campus for Mr. Simmons to interview prospective candidates. At first, Mr. Simmons wondered if he and the committee had made a mistake in deciding to call a recent seminary graduate as pastor. Some of the candidates he talked with came across with such timidity that he felt embarrassed for them. Still, others seemed more inclined toward a career in academia. "Is this the best Maylor has to offer?" He wondered.

Mr. Simmons was on the verge of going home when Davis walked in for his interview. Almost immediately, Davis won him over. Where others had seemed timid, Davis was confident. The only time Mr. Simmons detected hesitancy in Davis was when he began to talk about his undergraduate background. To Davis's surprise, Mr. Simmons considered his degree from Temple to be a plus. Mr. Simmons liked the idea of door-to-door witnessing, which he believed Independent Baptists were more inclined to do. Mr. Simmons ended the interview by telling Davis he was going to recommended him to the church as their next pastor.

First Baptist of Middleville flourished under Davis's leadership. He gained the confidence and support of both church and community leaders, especially Sam Jones. His financial backing allowed the church to build a new addition, a new youth center, and a new coffee house/theater ministry center.

Davis attributed his success to his willingness to stick to basics. He tried to model what he asked of his congregation by taking part in hospital visitation and door-to-door witnessing, even though the latter was beginning to fall out of fashion, even among Baptists. Davis also worked hard on his sermons, and this showed both in his delivery and the depth of what he shared on Sundays.

With the establishment of the church's anti-bullying program, Davis began to gain notoriety outside Middleville. The church's program received favorable write-ups in Southern Baptist periodicals as well as a feature article in the local paper. Yet Davis thought the church's program warranted more mainstream secular attention. But, as Davis well understood, the secular press (outside of Texas at least) was at best paternalistic to anything associated with evangelicalism, especially of the Baptist sort. Why the hostility? Davis often wondered. Davis was pondering this attitude of the press when his secretary interrupted to let him know it was time for his next appointment.

Davis warmly greeted Eian Braymore and offered him a seat in his office. He noticed Eian seemed somewhat ill at ease, so he quickly shifted the conversation to Eian's background.

"I understand you're from Plainsville. Pastor Cook was a classmate of mine at Temple," Davis began.

"Yes, he always spoke well of his time in Philadelphia," Eian responded. The mention of Philadelphia caught Davis off guard. It was not uncommon for those unfamiliar with Texas Temple to confuse it with Temple in Philadelphia. Davis wondered how Eian, having been a member at Plainsville, would confuse the two schools. Yet Davis pressed ahead.

"Normally, I ask those seeking membership in the church to share something of their faith. May I ask, how did you come to know the Lord?" Davis inquired.

At first, Eian seemed not to understand the question, but quickly recovered, and offered this response, "Reverend, I'm glad you asked that question. For me, really, the key was 9/11. It was on that day sitting at a lunch counter watching the video of that terrible attack with other patrons that I reached a turning point. I felt a spiritual kinship with humanity and our common struggle for life and wholeness. I sensed something lacking in me, and I then realized that I wanted to be a force for good in the world."

Davis was unsure of how to respond. Outside of a marriage license, he was rarely called Reverend. And he couldn't ever recall being called Reverend by a fellow Baptist. Eian's testimony, such as it was, did not give him a warm and fuzzy feeling about his faith. Davis began to wonder about Eian. Is he for real? He thought. "When you sensed this lacking in you, would you say that you then saw Christ as the answer to your spiritual ills?" responded Davis.

"Absolutely, Reverend, I saw Christ as a source of goodness and truth, beyond that of even spiritual leaders such as Gandhi and Martin Luther King," Eian answered.

In all his years of ministry at Middleville, Davis had never actually turned someone away who was seeking church membership. Davis was a theological conservative, but he tried to be as generous as he could be in understanding the unique way in which each person came to know the Lord. He didn't hold anyone to a formula for conversion. Yet, Davis knew that turning Eian away was, in fact, the necessary thing to do. Searching for a graceful way to say, "No," he stalled for time by asking another background question of Eian.

"What do you see as your life's vocation?" asked Davis.

Eian appeared more than ready for the question, and as he answered, Davis mostly forgot about his plans to refuse him church membership gracefully.

"I really see myself as called to be a writer. Although I'm a technical writer by profession with an IT firm in the area, I really have aspirations beyond that. I would like to break into journalism, and perhaps—I know this sounds ambitious—shape the way evangelical ministries, such as this one, are defined by the secular press," Eian responded.

Hearing this, Davis could only set aside any misgivings he had about Eian's faith. He would meet with him later to help him understand the Gospel. But if he turned him away, he would miss the opportunity to work with someone apparently of the same mindset as he was, with regard to the attitude of the secular press toward evangelicals.

"Well, I think I've heard all that I need to hear. As pastor of Middleville, I would like to warmly welcome you into our family of faith, Eian."

CHAPTER 3

Like many recent hires at Proteus, Eian seemed like an unlikely choice for the company. He was a sociology major with a good, but not especially standout, academic record at Brown. He had noticed an ad for "technical writers...open to all majors" on the department job board. The announcement also mentioned that, if selected, the company would pay for any student loans that had been taken out by the applicant. As he was finishing his B.A. with no job prospects in sight and mounting student loan debt, the Proteus job seemed ideal.

Eian sent Proteus his resume. Soon after, he received an email reply to report to an on-campus testing center for the next step in the application process. Eian arrived not knowing quite what to expect. He was asked to empty all his pockets and leave his belongings in a locker outside the facility. Upon entering he was asked to state his name, social security number, and then asked to look directly into a camera without blinking or moving his head. When he did this, a door opened into a small room with a computer terminal and a monitor.

He sat down at the terminal, and the test began.

"In this testing scenario, Eian, you'll be an online customer service representative, taking orders and responding to questions. For the first set of questions, we ask you to type your answer into the text box provided. After that, we would like you to speak your answers into the microphone provided."

The first set of questions were relatively easy. Eian began to gain a sense of confidence as he typed his answers. Things soon became more difficult. One person called and said he had received an email with a tracking number, but he deleted the email by mistake.

"Could another tracking number be generated?" he asked.

"Yes sir, I believe our tech support staff could fulfill that request," Eian responded. When asked how long it would take, Eian replied that the request would be handled in the order in which it was received.

So far so good, Eian thought. He then received an odd call from a woman who didn't have a comment or question about an order, but just wanted to hear a friendly voice. When she began breathing rather heavily into the phone, Eian, unsure of what to do simply said, "Ma'am, we seem to be having trouble with our connection. It was nice talking with you."

The next series of calls came from increasingly irate customers with all manner of complaints. Eian began to wonder if he was applying for a position in a psych ward, rather than an IT company. Yet with each call, Eian handled the wildest complaints with calm precision, which was exactly what Proteus was looking for. He was hired.

Eian was told via email to report for training at the Proteus Advanced Research Facility in Black Sands, New Mexico. As Eian traveled to the facility, he was glad to have landed the job and have his student loans covered by the company, yet he wondered if they only intended him to be a glorified clerk of sorts. He soon found out otherwise.

On the day of his arrival, an attractive female attendant escorted Eian to his room. It included all manner of conveniences and luxuries—a king-size plus bed, wine and cheese, fruit, snacks and coffee of endless variety, and a flat-screen TV that covered nearly the entire wall. The bathroom included an enormous shower and a huge separate tub with a large window looking out over the desert landscape. Eian could scarcely take it all in.

"Dinner will be served at 1800 in the second-floor dining room," the attendant informed Eian. "Should you care to change for dinner, clothing is available in the closet on your left," she motioned.

Eian thought of asking what 1800 signified in non-military time but thought better of it. He did venture to ask how the company knew his clothing sizes.

"Oh, from your recent online clothing orders. We hope you don't mind," replied the attendant. "We only seek out personal information online when it's in the best interest of those in our corporate family."

This explanation left Eian unsatisfied. But any misgivings he had about online privacy were overridden in this palatial room talking with this gorgeous attendant.

"No, I don't mind at all. Thank you for everything," Eian replied.

At 10 minutes till 1800, Eian was about to leave the room and make his way downstairs when there was a knock on the door. It was the attendant. She had changed into a black dress and asked Eian if he wouldn't mind if she accompanied him for dinner.

"How could I refuse?" he responded with a smile.

As Eian and his dinner date made their way into the dining room to their assigned seats, he glanced over the others in the room. To his surprise, all were male and appeared to be close to his age. Didn't Proteus make a big deal about diversity? He thought.

As the dinner conversation progressed, Eian surmised that the men sitting nearest him (with their equally attractive dates) were also liberal arts graduates from Ivy League schools. Though Ivy League, they were (he gathered) like him, not from affluent backgrounds, and were probably deeply in student loan debt before landing a job at Proteus, for which they seemed grateful.

That evening after dinner, Eian was instructed to report to the facility's main auditorium where he, along with the other trainees, would receive an introduction to the company from its CEO, William Whentworth. Along with other new employees, Eian could not have been more delighted about the prospect of hearing the world famous titan, Whentworth.

As he walked into the main auditorium, Eian was led to his seat by the same lovely female attendant who had been his dinner date. As they made their way to his assigned seat, she leaned into him and pressed a card with her extension into his hand.

"Call me after the meeting, and I'll come up to your room for a drink. I would love to hear all about you," she said. Eian could only turn and offer an embarrassed smile, while he pondered the implications of her offer.

His seat appeared to be part dentist chair and part space camp simulator. It could lean all the way back, and there was a huge headpiece. And there where places for his arms and legs to be strapped in. Eian took his seat with as much calm as he could muster. Whentworth soon arrived on the stage before him.

As Whentworth took the stage, Eian started to applaud but caught himself after noticing another trainee clapping wildly, yet being greeted with a sharp scowl from Whentworth. "No, my young guardians, don't applaud me. Let me applaud you," after which Whentworth clapped and bowed his head toward the audience. Whentworth then began his address, which Eian couldn't forget if he tried.

"My friends, we stand on the brink of a new era. You have been specially chosen to lead us into the new era. For the first time, we have the opportunity to combine all forms of communication (transmitted in electronic format) into one global enterprise, giving us control over all the information most people take in. Before going any further, however, permit me to offer an illustration which will help lend clarity to my further points. I would ask you all to lean back and remain perfectly still."

As he leaned back, Eian felt the headpiece slide completely over his head, blocking his vision in all directions. He also felt strapped into the chair at the hands, feet, and waist.

"Friends, forgive this inconvenience, but it will (I assure you) prove worthwhile," Whentworth began again.

Eian opened his eyes inside the headpiece and noticed a screen divided into three parts. The screens on the right and left displayed random images and words fed at random speeds. The screen in the middle displayed words or phrases fed at an even, slow pace.

"The images on the right and left before you," continued Whentworth, "represent reality as it's perceived by the public in our world. This reality is simply a random set of images they cannot make sense of. Our job is to turn their attention away from the images on the left and right, and focus their full attention on the center screen of reality, which we control."

Mention of the word "control" left Eian with a sense of uneasiness.

"By control, I don't mean we can manipulate people in some robotic way," continued Whentworth. "We simply provide people with what they want; well most of them, anyway. And what is that? In our world, the public is divided into three classes—the informed, the uninformed, and those off the grid.

"The informed, as Ellul has taught us, not only want propaganda, they literally need it, because they need an opinion about everything. We provide those opinions to them. Indeed, our task is to keep them trapped in an endless cycle of becoming more opinionated.

"The uninformed are only so to a degree in our day. Before the age of digital communication, it was possible (as C.S. Lewis well illustrated) for some to buy the paper to read the box scores, and nothing else, thereby leaving them unaffected by our propaganda. One cannot isolate oneself from the world outside sports and entertainment to that degree today. No one faced with the flood of information presented to them in the digital age can pretend to be oblivious to the news outside of sports and entertainment. Our job is to humor the uninformed and keep them trapped in an endless cycle of entertainment in which we can spoon feed them easily digestible bites of information tailored to our purpose. If we control the grid completely (which we will), no one will find a true escape from the larger world by taking shelter in amusements. They'll be given what we want them to believe through their amusements.

"And what of those who are off of the grid completely? Well, I'm afraid we lack control over them altogether. But that's a subject and a problem for another time."

It appeared Whentworth was nearing the end of his remarks, but yet he pressed on.

"Friends, before releasing the restraints on your seats (which I apologize for), I wanted to underscore a point related to them. These represent the restraints the public has chosen to impose on their reality. These keep them trapped in a cave of their own making in which you, like Plato's guardians of old, act as filters, interpreting and shaping their reality."

The restraints were released, and the seats reclined forward. Eian risked a glance around the room. Everyone appeared mildly shocked.

"I wanted to leave you with some final thoughts," Whentworth stated. "The key to tying our entire new enterprise together can be thought of in terms of the concept of the crowd, as taught to us by Le Bon. All of the public must be brought along slowly to be of one mind, subverting all logic and blurring all differences of class, religion (especially religion), race, or gender. It matters not where the public is located. They are part of the crowd—a living social animal.

"Some of you may wonder," Whentworth continued, "why the organization believes it has the right to act in this way. I'm afraid the task before us overrides question of rights or morals (however useful such teachings may have been to our ancestors). What lies before us, as Ellul well taught us during the atomic age, is necessary because it's possible. Possibility overrides any secondary concerns or any who object to the task before us.

"Before closing, no doubt some of you may have some misgivings about what you've heard," Whentworth noted. "That's natural, I assure you. If, however, you wish not to proceed any further in the training program, simply press the red button on your left armrest."

Eian waited. There was a deadly silence over the auditorium. Momentarily though, a beefy security guard appeared in the row above him. He held out a large hand to a nervous looking trainee, whom he led out a front side door. Eian felt himself sweating through his shirt.

"Well, I'm sorry not all of you will be proceeding with us," added Whentworth with a strained smile. "It's my hope the remainder of you (whom I assume are in agreement with what you've heard) will grow professionally in your time here and learn to enjoy your place in the organization. You have been given a rare opportunity. Don't waste it. Thank you for allowing me the privilege of introducing you to our corporate family."

Eian sat in his room typing a quick email to his parents, but words failed him. He knew his parents were delighted with the news of his new job, and especially with the news that his new employer would be paying off his student loans. Yet, Eian had to tell them something. So he quickly sent a short note about his wonderful accommodations and attached a picture of the room.

After sending the email, Eian lapsed into deep thought. Although raised attending church, he wasn't especially Christian. His professors had made sure of that. Yet he had retained from his upbringing enough of a sense of what was ethically right to realize that what he had just heard from Whentworth was coldly unethical. But what can I do? He wondered. Despite his Ivy League pedigree, his job prospects (with his major) were nil in this economy. And if he did quit, would the company renege on their student loan payoff offer? No, he had to find a way to reconcile things within himself and make things work.

As Eian sat lost in thought, there was a knock at the door. He answered.

"You didn't call, so I thought I would stop by to make sure everything was all right," said his lovely female attendant, as she played with her hair. "Well, aren't you going to invite me in?" She smiled as he invited her into the room.

Eian noticed her dress was even a tad shorter (as if that were possible) than the one she had worn at dinner. He tried to avert his eyes as she sat across from him. "How was your meeting?" she asked.

"It was a lot to take in, that's for sure. I'm still trying to sort through everything," he responded. "I don't know how long you've been with the company, but do you ever have any doubts about whether you're in the right place? I'm sure there is an opportunity for a career here, but I can't help but think if maybe I'm giving something of myself away (in an unethical way) to the organization."

As he talked, Eian glanced at her legs and noticed a scar on her upper thigh. Does she cut herself? He wondered. Mindful of the cameras and microphones which lined the room, she merely looked at him and smiled, while pulling her skirt down. As she did so, Eian caught her eye, and he knew she understood him.

"Say, with as much time as we've spent together, I don't even know your name, girl." She laughed and pulled her chair towards him. Reached for the remote control on the bed. Dimmed the lights and turned on some music. She put a finger to his lips with one hand and wiped a tear from her cheek with the other.

As the clock struck 0300, she sat on the edge of the bed and slipped on Eian's shirt, buttoning it up nearly all the way. No need to give the camera crew any cheaper thrills, she thought. She had to talk with Eian in private. Well, as privately as she could in a bathroom with microphones. But at least it lacked cameras! She slipped a room notepad and pen into her shirt pocket and leaned over to wake up Eian. He was sound asleep. "Eian, let's take a shower together," she said a couple of times. Eian finally came out of his slumber with a confused look. He started to roll over. She had waited until 0300 when she knew there would be a guard shift change. Still, the morning crew might review the tape. She would have to risk it.

"Follow me into the bathroom. Please, I need your help," she said as distinctly as she could into his ear. He leaned up on his elbow, eyes wide open, and nodded.

In the bathroom, she turned on the shower and pretended to take one with Eian. In between writing notes to Eian on a notepad, she ostentatiously gave audio instructions to Eian to put more soap on her back. He looked confused at first. She wrote as quickly as she could, explaining that the room and bathroom contained microphones. And that although the room contained cameras, the bathroom didn't. Eian slowly nodded. She then told him her name was Lin, and she was from China. She had been recruited by the company as a teenager from an orphanage with the promise of U.S. citizenship and having the company pay for her college education. At first, she was treated well. But after they had taken her dignity from her, they threatened her life if she left. She wanted out.

"Can I trust you?" she wrote. He nodded. "It's too risky for us to be together here any longer. I'll call you when you leave. Don't worry, it may take a while, but I'll find you," she wrote. She gave him a long kiss and quickly left his room.

CHAPTER 4

Eian had been in Middleville for over a month and had now seen much of the town. An office was being built for him in the technology co-location facility at the former Air Force base. When it would be finished and what he would actually do in the office, he had not yet been told. When he left the company training facility in Black Sands, he was given transportation to Middleville, where an apartment and car were ready for him. His instructions were to talk with as many people as possible in town and take notes and recordings of conversations.

In making these recordings, the organization had supplied Eian with a special belt lined with audio storage devices. Naturally, this belt was known within the organization as a Markov belt in honor of Russian mathematician Audrey Markov—a nineteenth-century forerunner of modern data science. Each year in June, Proteus commemorated Markov's birthday with a logo on its main page. The general public could be counted on to glaze over in silence at the mention of Markov's name. Few had heard of him, let alone knew he had a birthday in June. But this was precisely the point. Commemorating his birthday (and that of other such technical luminaries) each year served to underscore the knowledge gap between Proteus and the masses.

Along with gathering audio recordings of conversations, he was to immerse himself in evangelical culture by attending church-related events, reading evangelical literature, and join an evangelical church. In joining, Eian was told to adopt an evangelical cover story regarding his background and faith. Eian came to Middleville with no particular love for evangelicals. (His professors had ensured that too.) Yet, as with other things about the organization, Eian had difficulty with the ethics of passing himself off as an evangelical. Also, the more time he spent in Middleville, the more he saw the secular stereotypes of evangelicals fall by the wayside. However, whatever misgivings he had about the company and his assignment, he had to press on for Lin's sake convincingly.

Since she left him that morning at the training facility, there was not an hour that went by that he didn't think about her. She became his motivating force. He would, however, at times doubt himself. Was her story really true? He thought. Nonetheless, at most times, he still believed her and knew he had no choice but to try to help her. What that actually might mean, he wasn't sure. But even though he had only known Lin a short time, he already felt something approaching love for her.

Lin had said she would find him. Assuming that his company laptop, phone, apartment, and car were under watch, he resisted the urge to try to call her, search for her on the internet, or do anything that might alert the organization that he was in contact with her. She had seemed confident of locating him. How would she do it? He wondered.

Eian attended church at First Baptist each Sunday and even attended a Sunday evening service. He had not yet, however, attended a Wednesday evening service. Given his instructions from the company (and always thinking of Lin's best interest), he decided attending a Wednesday evening service would be the best use of his time.

Eian politely declined an after-church invitation to a church member's home that evening. He had been spending most evenings at a local diner and liked the feel of the place. He was even becoming known as something of a regular.

On his way out of the church that evening, he spotted a large wall of mail-slot-like boxes. This part of the church was normally quite crowded on Sundays, and Eian had not noticed the boxes. He now noticed there was a sign under a group of boxes labeled "New Members." Eian located his box. It was quite full of all sorts of items—coupons, business cards, fliers for church ministries, and an apparent assortment of other church-related materials. He gathered the whole stack on his way to the car.

At the diner, Eian sat the stack of church mail next to his laptop. "Chicken sandwich again tonight, honey?" the waitress asked. Eian nodded in the affirmative and smiled. Although he knew she called every male honey, he still enjoyed hearing it.

Eian began looking through what had been left in his church box. He opened a note from an apparent job hunter named Matt who was "looking for some advice on getting into the IT consulting business." Eian sorted through various restaurant coupons and church ministry materials. Near the bottom of the stack, he noticed a small envelope. He opened it and froze. He then looked slowly around the diner as he began to read.

"Eian, I'm sorry it's taken me so long to contact you. I didn't want to raise suspicion. My life is still under threat if I leave, and since I have no family, my friends here are now being threatened. I still need your help (and I know this may sound strange), but I really need you. And just so you don't wonder, this note came to you through a friend of a friend in Houston. Listen, the company is sponsoring the TechExpo event in Houston later in the year. I don't know any details at this point, but most likely, I'll be one of the girls making the trip. Let's meet that weekend. I'll reach out to you again when I can. Miss you and praying for us both, Lin."

"More coffee, honey?" Eian looked up startled. "You okay, honey?" He smiled and apologized then declined more coffee. Eian sat lost in thought for a moment. He then looked around and carefully concealed Lin's note between a stack of church announcements. He paid his bill and drove back to his apartment.

Eian could hardly sleep that night. His thoughts kept turning to Lin. Where was she? What was she doing? He also couldn't help but think about her mentioning that she was praying for the two of them. Eian couldn't remember a time in his life when he had prayed. Yet as he faded off to sleep, he prayed, "Dear God, wherever she is tonight and whatever she's doing, keep her safe."

A month passed. Eian began to grow restless. Finally, he received an email telling him his new office was ready. That morning he received a package at his apartment. It contained his ID card for accessing his office, located on what had been the former Air Force base.

Eian showed his ID to the guard at the gate, and then drove to his office. At first, he thought he had the wrong building. Nothing about it from the outside offered any indication of activity on the inside. There was only one other car in the lot. Eian rechecked the email the company had sent him. This was the place.

He was about to get out of the car when a man in a security guard's uniform approached the car.

"You, Eian?" the guard said as Eian stepped out of the car. "Welcome, we've been expecting you." The guard escorted Eian to the front of the building. He didn't notice an entrance. Yet as they approached the building, the guard opened a door, which seamlessly blended in with the rest of the building's front.

They walked inside and the door shut behind them. Eian looked around. Except for a desk occupied by the guard, the building seemed as unoccupied on the inside as it did from the outside.

"If you don't mind my asking, does anyone else work here? I mean, besides us?" Eian asked the guard.

"Officially, yes. There are servers in the basement owned by other organizations. But they would only be used in case of a power outage at another location," the guard responded.

Eian nodded before asking the guard where his office was.

"Down this hall to the right," the guard answered.

As Eian turned right at the end of the hallway, a door shut behind him. He hadn't noticed a door being there. As he turned around, a panel appeared on the wall in front of him.

"Welcome. Please verify your identity by first stating your name and social security number. Next, look directly into the camera before you," said a computerized female voice. Eian did as instructed. "Welcome, Eian. My name is Kari. Should you need anything at all, don't hesitate to ask. Allow me to show you around your new office." A door slid open, and Eian walked through it. As he did, the door closed behind him.

Kari proceeded to show him around the office. Eian was overwhelmed. He had imagined the office as a glorified cubicle with perhaps a little more privacy. This was part luxury hotel suite, part command center.

"On your left is the bathroom. And just off the bathroom is the kitchen. If you prefer any additional snacks, let me know. At the far end of the kitchen is the door leading to the bedroom," Kari continued. "There's a digital catalog of movies available on the bedroom TV, but if you're unable to find one you like, let me know."

After a tour of the bedroom, bathroom, and kitchen, Eian was directed to the main work area. He immediately noticed four clocks on the wall, keeping local time in Middleville, Washington, D.C., Beijing, and Black Sands. Kari continued her tour.

"The far left monitor is used for teleconferencing. I'll set that up for you when it's needed. The large monitor in the middle is used for your editing, and the monitor on the right is a live view of websites of interest to our project. I'll walk you through all you need to know, but ask me any questions you like."

Eian had not planned on staying the night at what he thought would be his office, not a second apartment. He decided to hold off on asking any questions related to returning to his apartment in town. Instead, he asked Kari about what he should do with the audio storage device that he had been instructed to bring with him.

"Glad you asked. Below the right monitor is a CPU tower with a USB cable attached to it. Plug this cable into the audio storage device. I'll take things from there." Kari went on to tell him that information on the storage device would be added to a project index, and that re-indexing would take about half an hour, after which a teleconference with project representatives in Black Sands would commence. Until then, Eian was to make himself at home.

The teleconference began as scheduled. Proteus representatives from Black Sands welcomed Eian to his new office. After which, they gave him an overview of the project. Project lead, Brad Van Doren started things off.

"Allow me to describe Project Evangel Blend. As the name implies, this project aims to blend evangelicals in with the rest of the population, removing some of the rougher edges of their faith, so they're normalized or more in keeping with mainstream society. The Achilles heel of the evangelical community is its desire for secular acceptance. Christian fundamentalists care little for such acceptance and even disdain it. Yet, despite Christ's woeful warning about all men speaking well of you, evangelicals covet the approval of the secular world. From our perspective (the secular one) this kindred desire is reflected on a cultural level. As has been observed, Chicago looks to New York and New York looks to Paris."

Eian was speechless. This office and all its technology were dedicated to this? At that point, Brad turned things over to the project technical lead, Ted Clayborne, but not without warning him not to get too far down into the technical weeds.

"Thank you, Brad. It's a pleasure to have you on board, Eian. After months of coding with my team, we're excited to fire up this beast. The core of the project is a massive set of indexes. Using the full text of books and articles from evangelical publishing houses, we scour the web to find every article related to evangelicals. These are then grouped by subject. We then parse these articles to find common word patterns. Next, I've taken the audio files that you and others have provided and converted these to text and then indexed them by category. We then combine all this data into a thought index. But not just any index. Here we take any characteristic evangelical thought and substitute a vague, platitudinous secular thought in its place. From these thoughts, we'll generate content for online comment boards, blog posts, fragments for social media, and full-fledged articles."

Ted asked if Eian had any questions. He did not.

"Very well then, if there are no questions, let's commence with the testing phase of the project. Eian, we've given the project the system name EB, short for Evangel Blend. To start things off, I invite you to ask EB a question (any question) related to faith."

Eian was almost stumped. The question put him on the spot, and Ted's attitude was off-putting. Ted resembled a parent observing a child taking his first steps. Eian composed himself and offered EB a question.

"Is it true there's a God?"

"Company policy mandates the separation of spirit and silicon," responded EB. This elicited a deep sigh of frustration from Brad and a look of surprise from Ted. Things were off to a shaky start.

Brad apologized to Eian. "We'll work this out. Won't we, Ted?"

Ted nodded nervously and rapidly. He set his team to work at once behind the scenes, while he reoriented the demonstration of EB on-the-fly.

"Instead of trying an example that may be too clever, let's try some working-level examples. Ones that should mirror how EB will function within the limits of this project," Ted responded.

"What we have in mind for EB on this project are what we term thought trees, which you'll help direct, Eian. Well, at least in the initial phases of the project. At the simplest level, EB will generate a comment designed for posting to social media or as a comment to an online article. The comment will be intended to subtly shift the emphasis of a point within evangelical theology from one of traditionalism to one more in keeping with mainstream society. For example, if an article takes a non-traditional view on abortion, EB will endorse this perspective with a comment something like: "The writer speaks for a growing number of evangelicals for whom the stale convictions of the past no longer hold sway. It's vitally important that evangelicals are known not simply as pro-birth, but better known for nurturing the whole life of the individual from a complete economic and social perspective from the birth to the grave."

"If you'll notice carefully," Ted continued, "a comment of this nature carefully avoids any interaction with the act of abortion itself nor the moral objections to it. Interacting directly with the morality of abortion (or homosexuality for that matter) will force immediate retrenchment on the part of evangelicals and those potentially sympathetic to their cause. No, we want to give evangelicals the impression that they are retaining their evangelicalism while shifting their beliefs in our favor. We never want to appear triumphant, as if we know better than they, although of course, we do. In time, they'll come to see that they now share our beliefs. They may look back with some regret as if they now remember Zion in the midst of Babylon, but their regret will come too late. Well, I'm getting too far afield and starting to sound more like Brad than the common-sense techie I fancy myself to be."

Ted received a quick note from his lead programmer explaining the initial glitch with Eian's question of God's existence to EB.

"It turns out that we forgot to turn off our default settings related to religious questions," Ted continued. "We'll give EB another attempt at your question, Eian. We are, however, anxious to set EB in motion online without further delay. To commence our efforts, I'll let EB take over from here. And he'll explain how and when he'll need your input, Eian."

Ted stepped away for a moment and then returned.

"It's all yours, EB," he stated.

With those words, the middle monitor jumped to life. EB quickly searched out articles online related to abortion and evangelicalism and then determined the one most favorable for posting an initial thought tree. He then generated and posted a comment remarkably similar to the one Ted had just presented. In fact, it was almost verbatim.

"Good morning, Eian," EB said. "Please indicate your agreement with my comment by pressing F1. Or to edit my comment, press F2. You may edit any of my comments at any time by pressing F2. Once you indicate your consent to my initial comment, it will move its way forward. Any of what I post online can (in cases of an emergency) be altered. We'll get to that."

Along with generating the initial comment, EB also generated one rebuttal and two posts affirming his comment. These added comments were all posted under different usernames (complete with personalized avatars) and appeared quite genuine to the unknowing online public. The rebuttal comment took the sharply secular tone typically encountered online wherever evangelical faith and social issues are discussed in an open secular forum.

"The problem is not getting evangelicals to alter their focus," the rebuttal comment read, "it's getting them to abandon their ridiculous faith altogether. Their book of bronze-age myths no longer has any relevance in the modern world. It has been overcome by events."

This rebuttal comment generated a response of agreement from a real-life poster. This comment was posted with the infidel bravado commonly encountered in such discussions. It read: "Could not agree more. Thank god, I'm an atheist!"

At this point, it seemed to Eian that EB was playing chess against himself and losing. Then EB posted this comment: "I understand your sentiments. My thought is that evangelicals are evolving like all of us. By all appearances, they are moving in a more favorable direction, which should be encouraged. Let's not slam the door in their faces."

EB quickly generated several plus votes for this last comment. In no time, no less than three flesh-and-blood posters shared their agreement. One commentator posted: "I can't help but agree. The sense I get from talking with younger evangelicals is that they're not interested in embracing the polarizing positions of their parents. They want a faith that speaks to their generation."

EB was programmed to generate comments, rebuttals, and plus votes on a site until the project objective was met. When it became clear that evangelical beliefs were now thoroughly blended with secular beliefs (and there was general consent to this on a site), he moved into monitoring mode for that site. Any new hostile secular comments or traditional evangelical ones were quickly deleted. They might appear to the user to have been posted at first but will in time disappear.

Proteus was able to maintain this tight level of control quite easily. The company now maintained a near-exclusive monopoly on nearly all social media, blogs, image and video sharing sites, discussion forums, and web-based email. To make one's voice heard online in almost any capacity now required a Proteus account.

Eian watched with amazement as EB's initial thought tree wound its way upward and outward over the next couple of hours. #ProLifeNotJustProBirth was now trending near the top of social media. EB even produced a slide-show presentation of some comments and posted it to the Proteus video sharing site, ProTube.

Ted and Brad could not have been more pleased with EB's progress. Brad thought, however, that he would pause EB long enough so Eian could again ask his initial question. "Eian has a question for you, EB," Brad said.

"How may I help, Eian?" EB replied.

"EB, is it true there's a God?" Eian asked.

"That's one of the primary questions of human existence. In Western culture, the biblical writers believed the heavens declare God's glory and what can be learned of God is plain from nature. Based on this knowledge, the Christian philosopher Thomas Aquinas observed that all things in the world are in motion. Yet this cannot be true of everything going back into infinity. There must exist at the beginning a first cause, an unmoved mover, or a God to set all other things in motion."

"EB has responded in fine, evangelical fashion," said Brad. "As with evangelicals, he's still at the young adult phase of his theological maturity in answering such questions, and his response reflects that limited growth. In no time, however, he will come to see (as we do) the limited vision of Aquinas and the Biblical writers. It isn't that one would attempt to logically disprove them. It's simply (as has been said) that the climate of opinion has changed to where one no longer views the world as they did. Yet, we don't want to rid ourselves entirely of the idea of a God or Christianity as a social institution. The Bible contains some useful stories for children and some helpful ethical principles for adults. And for the unlearned, Christianity can continue to serve a social utility as the opium of people. We who know better must abandon any pretense of faith in the supernatural. Our faith is now where knowledge lives and where it will come to be. Its day we can only yet imagine. Our generation may not live to see it. Yet EB will. He'll see that far off divine event foretold of old by Tennyson in which knowledge will be to all as an open book."

With these words, Brad became emotionally overcome and had to excuse himself for a moment.

"We all share Brad's passion for truth, Eian," said a grinning Ted. "I simply see us arriving there in a way that will seem more natural than apocalyptic. Yet get there we will. Science fiction, this is not. It's simply the application of current technology, taken as far it will go and beyond. EB will learn, and we'll learn with him."

Having recovered his emotions, Brad returned.

"Based on initial results, it appears that EB is growing and adapting at a rate we never thought possible. We would ask that you remain in the office for the remainder of the week, Eian. This weekend, though, continue to attend church and various meetings with evangelicals. We'll know for sure that the project is having its intended effect on the public when we hear EB's words repeated back to us, especially from evangelicals themselves."

Brad and EB signed off. Ted instructed Eian to make himself at home and not hesitate to call on Kari should he need anything at all. Eian smiled until Ted signed off.

Kari was in a talkative mood after having to stay in mute mode on Eian's first day. "Well that was certainly a lot to take in for one day wasn't it?" Kari asked.

"Yes, it was. My head hurts," Eian responded.

Can I get you some aspirin or something to drink or eat?" Kari responded.

Eian indicated he would accept all three and thanked her. Kari went to work in the kitchen. Eian sat lost in thought as he ate the sandwich she had prepared. If he had not seen with his own eyes what he had just witnessed, he would not have believed it possible. He had been prepared for an online study of evangelical attitudes.

That he could understand. This was more like a paranoid fantasy—part Frankenstein and part Stepford Wives. It was as if the company wanted to bring to life an online social animal, and yet not merely bring it to life for its own sake, but to manipulate the beliefs of every person coming into contact with it. It was like a computer virus. Worst of all, the project entailed no financial benefits to Proteus. The project aimed at altering public opinion in a secular direction because it was possible and deemed desirable. Eian recalled a passage of Dostoevsky he had read in college. Standing in the Crystal Palace, representing the height of 19th-century technological optimism, Dostoevsky believed that only through great internal spiritual resistance could he resist the power of Baal or the belief that the here and now is all there is. Eian wondered if he had the inner resources to resist.

"Could I get you anything else?" Kari asked.

"Thank you, Kari. I'm fine," he responded.

Kari once more seemed in a talkative mood and asked Eian several questions about his family and his interests.

"So, tell me, is there a special someone in your life?" she asked.

Eian was taken aback. For the first time since he could remember, Lin had not been at the center of this thoughts. EB's demonstration had so overwhelmed him that he could think of nothing else at the moment. He quickly recovered.

"Not right now. Since starting with the company, I've been so busy that I don't have time to date," Eian responded in a less-than-convincing tone.

"Well, I'm sure there's someone out there for a nice young man like you," Kari responded.

After Eian faded off to sleep for the night, Kari generated a quick email to headquarters at Black Sands. The email read: "Eian apparently has a special someone in his life. Haven't been able to find out who or where she is. I'll keep my eyes and ears open, though."

CHAPTER 5

That Sunday morning Eian decided to attend the college and career Sunday school class. He had not previously attended the class and was unsure what to expect. He filed into the back of the large classroom a few minutes before the class began.

He was warmly greeted by those around him and even invited out for lunch after the service. Towards the front of the room, Eian noticed the class teacher, Roger Crabtree. Eian identified him from his picture on the church website. Pastor Crabtree had been ministering at First Baptist for two years as Pastor of Youth and Student Ministries.

Clad in a mock turtleneck and wearing a headset microphone, Pastor Crabtree moved to the center of the front of the large classroom.

"Good Morning, y'all," the pastor said as he scanned the entire room. "Oh, my! Let's try that again," he continued. "Good Morning, y'all. That's better. I thought I was in the seniors' class."

After engaging in a little more jocularity with the class, Pastor Crabtree began his lesson for the morning.

"All things to all people. That is our focus this morning." He then led the class in an opening prayer and went on with his lesson.

"I'm sure many of you have had the experience of getting clothing altered," the pastor continued. "What happens when we take, say, a pair of pants in for alterations? Well, we alter the garment, so it fits us better than it did before. We still have the same garment. It just fits us better now. Our faith is that way. There may be times where we need to adjust it or alter it, so it fits our intended audience better."

Eian was having trouble focusing on the pastor's lesson. His mind headed in various directions. As the pastor continued, Eian quickly regained focus.

"I had the opportunity this past week to participate in an online study with several pastors and student leaders. A topic that came up repeatedly in our discussions was how we can reach our generation, the younger generation, with the Gospel. Statistically, it's no secret that young people are turning away from the faith in ever-increasing numbers. How can we reverse that trend? Why aren't young people turning to faith in the way their parents did? The key point we arrived at in our online discussion is that the message of the Gospel needs to be tailored, so it speaks to the younger generation. The social issues that motivated our parents' generation no longer speak to this generation."

Pastor Crabtree, Eian observed, at this point in the lesson seemed to be thanking the older generation for its service, as one would recognize returning combat veterans. The pastor soon turned his attention back to the younger generation.

"To reverse the trend of young people abandoning the faith, we have to speak to our generation in its language. We have to let them know we're not just pro-birth, we are pro-life. We embrace all life. We believe in sheltering the homeless, caring for the earth, and defending the rights of the oppressed. These are the types of issues our generation understands, and when we focus on these issues, we become all things to our generation. Let us pray. Father, may we be as trees planted by the rivers of water, providing shelter to those outside our fellowship (especially those of our generation), drawing them in and reminding them that we are not just pro-birth but pro-life in the full sense. May we embrace all living things and foster justice and healing. In Jesus' name we pray. Amen."

Eian was floored. He had recorded the pastor's words. No doubt Brad and Ted would be delighted. They had stressed to him that if catchphrases were repeated often enough online, the public would eventually adopt them. It didn't matter that the logic of "pro-life, not just pro-birth" could easily be challenged. Logic made no difference to the crowd. Nor did truth, since all effective propaganda was based on truth. This subtle challenge to pro-life beliefs (Ted and Brad would say) represented an example of applying Ellul's propaganda principle of "truth, out of context."

Two months passed. During this time, Brad and Ted had instructed Eian to participate in what they termed the PR phase of Project Evangel Blend. This phase of the project would commence with two articles, both of which would laud Brother Davis and the anti-bullying ministry of First Baptist of Middleville. One of these articles appeared in Houston—a magazine distributed throughout Texas, as well as serving as an in-flight and complimentary hotel magazine in and around Houston. The other article appeared in the religion section of the Dallas Evening News, which had a wide online readership and subscribers throughout the South. Eian interviewed Brother Davis for both articles and supplied the first drafts. A team of Proteus writers working with Brad and Ted reworked Eian's first drafts. Another company team generated commendatory letters to the editor of both publications as well as a slew of anonymous donations to First Baptist, designated to the anti-bullying ministry.

Brother Davis was overwhelmed by the response to both articles. It was far beyond anything he had anticipated. He couldn't thank Eian enough. Based on the favorable response to both articles, Davis hatched the idea of a regional ministry conference focused on the theme of anti-bullying.

On a sunny afternoon, Davis sat in his office organizing the anti-bullying crusade with his secretary, Gail McBride. The pair worked out various details such as a conference fee, speakers' fees, and an overall conference theme, with Pastor Crabtree supplying his input via text. Davis and Miss McBride were focused on finalizing the speakers' bios when the phone rang. "It's Sam Jones, Brother Davis."

"Sam, it's good to hear from you," Davis said.

"I know you're busy, so I won't be long. I just wanted to let you know I couldn't be prouder of you and all you're doing in Middleville. I understand you're putting together a conference addressing the same themes as in those recent articles. Rest assured you have my full support. Let me know how I can help."

"Thank you, Sam. You've faithfully supported us in so many ways over the years. And if that's something you feel led to do again in this case, we would welcome that support."

"I'm glad to do it, Brother Davis. Tell me though. I noticed that a freelance writer, Eian Braymore wrote both of the recent articles about the ministry. How did you become acquainted with this fella?"

"Eian is a member here at the church. In fact, when he joined he expressed an interest to me in using his writing talents to help share this ministry with the secular world."

"Well, he has certainly done that. The articles even seem to be attracting a lot of attention on the internet," Jones added.

"Yes, Eian works for Proteus here in town as a technical writer. He probably used some of his computer skills to help promote the articles on the internet," Davis added.

Jones again congratulated Davis on the well-deserved notoriety the anti-bullying ministry (and his ministry in general) now seemed to be receiving. As he ended the call, however, Jones couldn't help but wonder about this Eian Braymore fella. He knew about Proteus's business presence in Middleville. His company leased them their buildings on the former Air Force base. It surprised him, however, to hear that a company technical writer would be employed at one of them. Jones had only the vaguest understanding of IT and didn't care to improve his knowledge in the area, but he understood (or at least he thought he did) how a server farm would operate. It would require an IT technical staff to monitor and at times power down and troubleshoot the servers. Technical writers might be needed elsewhere (perhaps at company headquarters) but not in buildings dedicated to servers.

While Jones did call to offer his congratulations and support to Davis, he also called to find out more about Eian. To be able to generate the publicity buzz that now seemed to surround Davis, Eian had to have connections with one of the big PR firms in Houston or Dallas.

Jones considered PR a necessary part of business. And he could always out-do the other guy in terms of publicity. Yet Jones also knew PR could generate limited returns or even losses if it was not carefully planned and managed. To generate the kind of buzz now surrounding Davis would take an effort that would require more than one person to accomplish. Yet that's what this Eian fella seemed to have achieved. Or did he? Jones continued to wonder, but he let the matter drop for the time being.

Back in his office, Davis could not have been in a better mood. The anti-bullying ministry he had started with little fanfare was now receiving recognition statewide. The planned conference would bring the ministry even more attention, perhaps as a model for others to emulate throughout the nation.

As Davis was lost in these thoughts, he looked down and noticed he had received an email from Pastor Heath Hodge. He was one of the pastors to whom he had extended an invitation to speak at the upcoming conference. Davis read the email with mounting dejection:

Jack,

Hope all is well in Middleville. I continue to hear good things about your ministry. And I'm honored to have been asked to participate in the upcoming conference.

As much as I would like to take part in the conference, I regret that I have a prior commitment. I'm scheduled to be at Scott Davidson's church that weekend.

Perhaps we could reconnect in person sometime in the spring.

Heath

Davis tried hard to suppress his disappointment. But he couldn't help himself. Heath Hodge was his link with the middle-aged, restless, and Reformed contingent within the Southern Baptist Convention. Because of his Independent Baptist roots, Reformed Baptists had always viewed Davis with a jaundiced eye. He recalled that Heath and Scott Davidson had been undergraduate classmates at Heaton. This memory left him feeling that despite all of his new-found notoriety, he still didn't quite measure up to Heaton standards.

The anti-bullying conference was a three-day event, beginning Friday and ending with Sunday services at Middleville. Workshops and sidebars were covering a range of issues from preventing school violence to monitoring social media. In these sessions, local officials stressed the need to involve students, parents, teachers, police, and clergy in the prevention of bullying.

Instructed by Proteus officials, Eian attended as much of the conference as he could. He interacted with as many conference participants as possible, all the while recording conversations. Eian couldn't help but be impressed with a large part of what he heard.

Many of the conference attendees were youth or youth pastors. In conversations with these youth pastors, Eian often found himself nodding in agreement.

"For too long," one pastor noted, "the church has been in reaction mode when it comes to the issue of bullying. We're reduced to the role of grief counselors after an incident of school violence occurs. We have to partner with the community in preventing these incidents from happening in the first place."

As much as Eian found himself in agreement with much of what he heard, he was snapped back into computer-generated reality by statements from several conference participants. While all seemed to agree the church needed to lead in school violence prevention and not merely react to it, many appeared to promote the idea that the church had been at fault for focusing on the wrong issues. Speaking for the many, one youth pastor noted, "that instead of helping to prevent school violence, evangelicals have been busy on the sidelines marching in pro-life rallies and promoting ballot initiatives on marriage. We should be known for embracing all of life, not just birth and marriage."

The conference ended with a Sunday morning sermon from Brother Davis. Although Eian had heard Davis preach several times already, the crowd gathered for this service was by far the largest. Eian settled into his seat near the middle of the sanctuary.

A man sitting next to Eian said he was "worried" Davis might have an invitation at the close of the service. Eian looked at the gentleman with surprise.

"You're not an Arminian?" the man asked.

Eian momentarily thought the question referred to ethnicity, but then vaguely recalled reading something about Arminianism versus Calvinism.

"Not really," Eian responded, "but some of my relatives are Nazarene."

"I'm sure you keep them in prayer," the man responded.

Eian was on the verge of a chuckle before he noticed the gentleman's concern was serious.

"Well, we're all in need of prayer," Eian added. The man nodded in agreement.

The morning service began shortly thereafter. Brother Davis strode to the pulpit to begin his sermon. Eian would remember it long afterward.

"I want to thank everyone who took time to travel to Middleville this weekend," Davis began humbly. "The theme of this conference is not a new one to you or this ministry. This weekend, however, we have laid bare this problem for an entire region to see. And I believe for the entire country to see.

"The problem of bullies and bullying is an old one. It's one our Savior experienced. He was ridiculed for who He was. He didn't fit in well with the popular crowd of His day. They mocked Him. They threatened Him. And they eventually plotted to kill Him.

"Our Savior was ridiculed throughout His ministry. Some of you may have been bullied throughout your young lives. How should you respond to this? There are many practical ways to seek help from classmates, parents, pastors, and others, as we've heard this weekend. And I encourage you to pursue those avenues in your community.

"Even in the most supportive environment, the problem of bullying (for the bullied and those who bully) is fundamentally a spiritual one. For those who are bullied, the problem eventually becomes one of forgiveness. That's something we can't do on our own. God must grant us that ability. The ability to not hate or withhold retaliation against those who revile us is unnatural to us.

"A good illustration of the Christ-like mindset we all should strive to cultivate is found in Dostoevsky's novel The Idiot. Its main character, the Prince, is one who is bullied. He also pursues the love of a woman. She not only doesn't return his love but is abusive to him. In spite of this, the Prince doesn't stop loving her, nor does he retaliate against others who revile him.

"The Prince points us to Christ Himself. He was reviled but didn't retaliate. He extended His love to those who didn't love Him, even those who abused Him. As Luke shares in his account of the Crucifixion, Christ asked the Father to forgive those who didn't know what they were doing, even as they were doing it, and even as they continued to do it.

"As the writer Walter Kaufman points out, there can't be a Christian tragedy. And this is so true. The death of Christ was not tragic. It was a triumph of love. God's love extended to us, the ungrateful. Whether we've bullied or been bullied, we need to be forgiven, and we need to forgive. The love of God granted to us by grace through Christ brings us that forgiveness."

The response to the conference online was nearly all positive. Southern Baptist blogger, Allan Cole, Jr., called the conference a "grace-filled response to a problem the church can no longer ignore." Progressive evangelical blogger, Rachel Weld Evergreen, was similarly enthusiastic, calling Davis "a leading voice for a new direction in the evangelical world." Upon publishing her lavish praise of Davis and the conference, Evergreen was surprised to find her blog post trending on social media.

After the conference, Davis found himself fielding several requests for interviews and media appearances. The most significant of these requests came from Ethan Hillberry, chief writer for the *Gotham Times Magazine*. He phoned Davis's secretary and set up an appointment time for a conference call interview.

Davis was enthusiastic about the interview. In fact, he nearly had to pinch himself to think that his ministry was receiving the attention of mainstream secular media to the degree that it now was. It was all happening so fast.

Davis sat his office on the day of the interview eagerly awaiting the call. It came about ten minutes late, causing him to fret that somehow there had been a change in plans. But the call finally came.

"Hello, Reverend Davis? This is Ethan Hillberry from the *Gotham Times*. I apologize for my tardiness. I had to take a phone call regarding the interview. We've decided to make your anti-bullying work the subject of a cover story."

Davis accepted Hillberry's apology and expressed his delight that the interview would be the subject of a cover story.

"What will be the headline for the story?" Davis asked.

"At the moment our working title is 'The New Face of Evangelicalism.' It will describe the mainstream aspects of your work," Hillberry responded.

Davis was not entirely comfortable with the headline or with the word "mainstream." He wanted his ministry to gain acceptance for meeting needs, not for its palatability or novelties. Yet he coveted approval and notoriety, especially the kind that a *Gotham Times Magazine* cover story would bring. So, he responded simply to the suggested title with "I see. Well, I'll certainly look forward to seeing that."

In the initial part of the interview, Hillberry asked Davis a series of general questions about the ministry. He also asked Davis a set of general questions about his background. Throughout this phase of the interview, Hillberry was highly complementary to Davis, heaping praise on him and his ministry for meeting vital needs in society.

Hillberry soon changed his tack.

"Reverend Davis," he said, "a story about a Southern Baptist minister is not normally the type of thing that would find its way into the pages of a publication like the *Gotham Times Magazine*, let alone as a cover story. I'm afraid that in order to proceed with publication of the story, we'll need something that will appeal to our readership."

Davis was taken aback. Why the put-down? The interview had been going so well, he thought.

"What do you have in mind?" responded Davis.

"To our readers," said Hillberry, "the concept of bullying is linked with other issues. I'd like to bring those into focus for this story. That being said, let me explore some ideas with you."

"As a minister," Hillberry asked, "you provide counseling to parishioners. Do you not?"

"Yes, that is part of our ministry," Davis answered.

"I see. Now in this part of your ministry (as you call it), do you personally provide counseling to gay and lesbian youth?" Hillberry asked.

"I have on occasion talked with a young person struggling with that," Davis responded.

"It is sad that you would see same-sex attraction as something to struggle with. There is a suitcase full of prejudice there. Nonetheless, in your counseling ministry, have you ever counseled anyone struggling with thoughts of suicide?" Hillberry asked.

"Yes, I have. Generally, however, except in crisis situations, I refer those dealing with suicidal thoughts to counselors with whom the person can receive more trained help," Davis said.

"Excellent," Hillberry responded. "Since you've counseled both gay and lesbian youth and parishioners dealing with suicidal thoughts, for our story, I'd like to invent a composite parishioner—a gay youth who suffers from suicidal thoughts related to his sexuality. Mind you this isn't a true journalistic composite, but it will serve the interests of our readers. Are you comfortable taking the story in this direction?"

Davis was decidedly uncomfortable. He would be going along with what was essentially a lie. But he rationalized by lying to himself. Thousands, perhaps millions of people might be reached by our ministry if this story is published. Who am I to deny them? And so he agreed to it.

"Yes, if that's the approach to the story, I'll go along with that," Davis answered.

"Wonderful. I believe that I have enough to work with to get started on the story. But before I go, let me dig a little deeper. If, hypothetically, you were to counsel a gay youth dealing with suicidal thoughts related to his sexuality, what approach would you take? Specifically, what might you say to him?" Hillberry asked.

Davis responded knowing that what he said in answer to this question would find its way into the story in some form.

"My first concern would be for his welfare," Davis responded. "I would try to remind him of God's love for him. And that God loves us all equally and unconditionally, regardless of who we are."

"That's very good, Reverend," Hillberry responded in the tone of voice of a teacher rewarding a student for providing the correct answer to a math question. "I just have a couple more questions. First, would you agree there are different interpretations of the Bible on the issue of homosexuality?"

Davis regretted he had ever agreed to the interview. He didn't want to be perceived as a theological liberal by questioning the traditional interpretation of the Bible related to homosexuality. His instincts told him to end the interview. But he had allowed it to go this far. He had to respond.

"Yes, it's my perception there are various interpretations of scripture on this issue. However, it's the belief of evangelicals like me that the Bible forbids us from acting on same-sex desires."

"I see," Hillberry responded. "I'm not sure our readers are interested in an intramural debate among Christians. For our story, it is sufficient to say you recognize there are different interpretations of the Bible on the issue of homosexuality."

Davis knew he should offer a rebuttal, but he remained silent. His head now hurt. He was angry with himself.

"If I may ask one more related question, Reverend. I appreciate you giving our readers so much of your time. Would you say issues like homosexuality and abortion are the main focus of your ministry?"

Davis was beside himself. To answer yes, would label him as the kind of right-wing reactionary liberals loved to hate. To answer no, would imply that he thought these issues were 'off to the side' and of little consequence. Something he firmly disbelieved. Yet he hedged his response.

"Well, I wouldn't say these issues are our main focus. My belief is it's important for evangelicals to be known for what we're for, not what we're against. I've always thought the people to whom we minister are more important than our theological positions."

"Reverend, I think our readers will enjoy reading about a minister guided by such thoughtfulness. Thank you for allowing me this much of your time. I'll send you the first draft of our story. Have a pleasant afternoon."

The story appeared in the magazine three weeks later. The cover featured a smiling young female wearing a #ProLifeNotJustProBirth t-shirt under the caption, "The New Face of Evangelicals." The story became a sensation online.

Drawing quick reactions were the portions of the story typeset in bold, large font, and set off from the rest of the article. "Like a growing number of evangelicals, Reverend Davis embraces a holistic view of ministry, not one narrowly focused on birth and sexuality," one highlighted portion read. While still another read, "Davis embraces the diversity of biblical interpretation on human sexuality."

What ultimately drew the most attention (and would raise the most questions) in the article were these words: "Davis once counseled a young person. I'll call him Bradley. He suffered from suicidal thoughts related to his sexual identity. Instead of offering Bradley condemnation, Davis represented Christianity at its best by reassuring this anguished soul of God's love for all of us regardless of our identities as individuals."

The reaction on the evangelical blogosphere was nearly immediate. On the liberal front, Rachel Weld Evans hailed Davis as "on track to be included in the litany of saints. Those individuals whose lives are a testament to the dynamic, all-embracing love of Christ." Holding the traditional line, Allan Cole, Jr., praised Davis for handling "that most difficult of all counseling situations with grace and wisdom." Yet, Cole "feared that Davis was fostering (perhaps unknowingly) a less-than-air-tight theology on one of the most important social questions of our day."

The article attracted widespread attention outside the evangelical world. Pop star Lady GooGoo propelled this by heaping lavish praise on Davis on social media. Before offering her millions of fans a link to the article and encouraging them to read it, she wrote that "This is the rare preacher willing to stand with my little outcasts. He has my love and support." And with it, Davis quickly garnered additional online support from a "who's who" of celebrities in the entertainment and sports industries.

Within a matter of weeks, Davis received an invitation from President Warren to speak at the White House Prayer Breakfast. A few days later came a speaking invitation from Harvard Divinity School. What perhaps gave Davis the most satisfaction was a conference participation request from Heaton College, which he declined because he had prior commitments this academic year.

When he looked back on how far he had come in such a brief span of time, Davis could scarcely believe it. His ministry and even his name were now known far and wide. Sure he had a few evangelical naysayers. These though, he convinced himself, were motivated more by envy than concern for orthodoxy. He was where he had always longed to be. Nothing and no one now stood in his way.

CHAPTER 6

Becky Worthington moved to Middleville with her father not long after the *Gotham Times* published its story on Brother Davis. In fact, it was reading about Davis and his ministry that reassured Becky's father, Darren, that he was making the right decision in relocating to Middleville from the suburbs of Houston.

Becky's mother had left her and her father when she was only a toddler. Her father had raised her and eventually began working at home so he could homeschool her. Darren enjoyed his life with his daughter in the Houston area.

He had enjoyed his work as a stockbroker; however, he recently made some wrong-way bets in the market with two of his long-time clients. Unable to recover his losses, he eventually had to concede defeat and acknowledge what happened to his clients. He lost their business, and news of their losses spread, resulting in other clients taking their business elsewhere. He needed a fresh start. A long-time client advised him to consider relocating to Middleville and offered to recommend him as a broker to friends living there.

The more Darren read about Middleville and its now famous pastor, the more he felt like moving there would be a good fit for him and his daughter. The town seemed to value faith and family, and it was away from the bustle of the Houston area. Darren also felt safe with the idea of sending Becky to public school in Middleville. He thought she needed to make a transition from homeschooling to being with other kids her age before going to college.

Shortly after arriving in Middleville and getting settled in a rental house, Darren decided to visit First Baptist with Becky. They were impressed with the preaching of Brother Davis and with the friendliness of the people. They decided to join the church.

Becky and her father received a tour of the church on the Sunday of their visit. As it happened, Alex Morgan was taking his turn in helping out with the church sound and video system. Alex held his smile a bit too long when meeting Becky. He scolded himself and then became irritated with himself for scolding himself. Alex would see Becky and her father at church several times before the start of the school year, but he remained too socially awkward to know how to approach her.

On the surface, Middleville High School appeared quite atypical. It stood almost entirely free from the drug and teen pregnancy problems plaguing many schools. And whereas even the simplest prayer or reference to the Creator might invoke the threat of legal action in some schools, Christianity (even evangelical Christianity) was quite common at Middleville High.

It was in the way this Christian faith took shape that gave the school its unique social structure. Typical of most schools, lunchroom seating signified a rigid social structure. One side of the lunchroom was known as "the sinner's side" and the other side known as "the missionary side." A middle portion of the lunchroom was known as "Purgatory." Students known to be involved in after-school Bible study or church ministries sat on the missionary side. Athletes, cheerleaders, and the generally more popular students sat on the sinner's side. The middle section attracted students involved in music, art, theater, and an assortment of video game and comic book enthusiasts.

This social stratification carried over to life outside the lunchroom. The honor of serving as Homecoming Queen typically went to a gal from the sinner's side. When after three years running, a student from the missionary side was selected, it did not escape notice. In her acceptance speech, the unlikely queen thanked the students, her parents, her teachers, her grandparents, and the Lord, all before inviting students to join her for after-school Bible study. She was greeted by fake smiles from the girls on the sinner's side, many of whom muttered terrible things about the Queen between their teeth. The boys on the sinner's side were equally cool to the Queen's speech. "We had to sit there and listen to Miss Missionary Side go on," one student remarked. Other sinner's side lads, condescendingly viewed the queen as something of an affirmative action selectee.

Dating and the question of whom one might socialize with generally followed the unwritten grouping rules established in the lunchroom. On all sides, some students had the traditional boyfriend, girlfriend relationships. Others preferred to cluster in groups with no two people declared to be a couple.

Before coming to Middleville as a senior, Becky's dating experience had primarily been of the teen group variety, although not entirely by choice. As Becky turned her father's approved dating age of 16, a book True Oneness by Joshua Hainsworth became all the rage in her homeschooling group. In his book, Hainsworth characterized dating outside of marriage as a "false oneness," and singles should "court" in preparation for marriage, but were not to date. Darren generally agreed with the theological slant of those in his daughter's homeschooling group. In this case, however, he found himself scratching his head. He let it slip to a group parent that he looked forward to Becky growing up and entering her dating years. "She's not going to save herself for marriage?" was the reply. He did a slow burn. He hoped by moving to Middleville that he could escape such narrowness and Becky could socialize in an environment better suited for teenagers.

Alex socialized in a group setting, mainly with kids from the Purgatory section of the lunchroom. He was not opposed to the idea of traditional dating; he just had not met his match. He was also quite busy.

A key component of Middleville's anti-bullying program was the monitoring of student postings on social media. Initially, a group comprised of school and police officials contracted with a local IT firm to design a social media monitoring system. Once delivered, however, the system met only the minimum requirements stipulated by the contract with the city. The system was better than not having one at all, but it fell far short of expectations. Alex volunteered to write an improved monitoring system. He was greeted with polite skepticism, but in the end, community officials thought they had little to lose by giving Alex the opportunity. He set to work.

Unlike the system the city had purchased from the local contractor, Alex's system was not centered merely on an index of terms students might use on social media, which might be perceived as offensive or threatening towards other students. Using what students posted about themselves, together with what he knew about the social structure of school life, Alex's software gathered information about each student into a student profile. This consisted of the social group the student belonged to, his friends within the group, and how long the student had belonged to that group.

Using this student profile, Alex would gather posts and group these by topic. Gradually, he trained his software to topically and stylistically index each post. He found that students discussing gaming generally used all lower case and were partial to monosyllable words. He also discovered that students discussing football were partial to all caps and exclamatory sentences.

Rather than looking for what might be deemed threatening or offensive, Alex's software focused on student profiles and posts failing to conform to established patterns. Thus, when a student not identified with any group began posting judgment of God passages from Isaiah (eschewing all caps and all lowercase), Alex's software was altered to the anomaly.

Alex notified his math teacher who notified the principal, who called the police. The police obtained a warrant for the student's cell phone records, which led to a search of the student's home. There the police found a weapons stash, a map of the lunchroom, and a virtual hit-list of students. Alex had helped to avert what might have been a horrific tragedy.

With the proven capability of Alex's software with helping to prevent a real-life threat to the community, the city hired him as a consultant. His task was to continue to improve his software. He was given a budget, office space in town and all the computer equipment he needed.

Alex was able to do well in school without too much effort or time. Still, his work for the city and his involvement at church left him with little time to socialize. This worried Alex's father, Drew, who was proud of his son's work with the community. Yet he didn't want Alex to miss out on the experience of being young by starting his work life too early.

Knowing nothing of her father's business troubles, Becky was a bit surprised by his suggestion that they relocate to Middleville. It was okay with her. Having been homeschooled all her life, she was ready for a new experience. She anxiously looked forward to the idea of going to a public school, like most other kids.

Becky found herself quite overwhelmed by the social scene at Middleville. Nothing had prepared her for it. For the first time in her life, she suffered from social anxiety, sometimes quite acutely. To mask this, she would go without her glasses so that she couldn't read people's faces as well. If this failed, she would affect a bored persona, so as not to appear overly interested.

She quickly became aware of the lunchroom social hierarchy, but couldn't quite find her place in it. Her appearance in the church choir made her a candidate for the missionary side; her interest in literature and music made her possible Purgatory material; her attractiveness appealed to the sinner's side. She became the rare student who could sit almost anywhere in the lunchroom without inviting mockery.

After church on Sunday evenings, Becky would socialize with the other kids at the church's Youth Activity Center. It was a large complex with a gym on the ground level, a game room upstairs, and meeting rooms in the basement. Becky and her father were impressed the church had gone to such lengths to provide a place where the church's youth could congregate.

A few weeks into the school year, Becky went to the Youth Activity Center after church on Sunday night. She followed some other kids who were heading upstairs. Once there, she looked around confused and uncertain of which group of students to approach. Some were grouped around pool tables; others were fixated on ping-pong or video games.

As she reached up to remove her glasses before approaching anyone, she noticed someone approaching her.

"Hi, Becky? It's great to see you here. I'm Heather Swanson. Come join us," she said as she motioned to a group of kids gathered around a pool table, surrounded by a throng of underclassmen.

As Becky quickly grasped, Heather and her friends were part of the in-crowd at school. Although Becky had only been in school a short time, she recognized three of the boys—Jeff Taylor, Tad Smith, Matt Nelson—as star football players. Heather seemed to be everywhere Jeff and the other boys were in school. The other girls—Lisa Salisbury and Nicole Martin—seemed to grudgingly follow Heather's lead. Tad and Matt were clearly followers of Jeff. For the privilege of standing near the group, the underclassmen would fetch soda refills, applaud success on the billiard table, and generally lend a supportive role.

When Becky and Heather approached the group, Jeff was lining up a shot. He paused momentarily and looked directly at Becky and smiled. Becky felt all eyes on her. She offered an embarrassed smile, turning quickly to Heather, who offered a look of approval.

After sinking the shot and being greeted by applause, Jeff walked over to Becky and introduced himself.

"I've seen you around, but I just haven't had the privilege of meeting you. Let's hear about you," he said, motioning towards a table.

Jeff pulled Becky's chair out for her and seated himself across from her. The other upperclassmen followed.

"Can I get you anything to drink?" Jeff asked.

"Oh, I'm fine. Thank you, though," Becky answered.

As Jeff sat across from Becky, he appeared to her as a model of male attentiveness. He listened and responded readily, but did not appear too eager. Perhaps the stereotypes about football players and sinners side males were overblown, she thought.

Becky thought Heather and the other girls were also surprisingly interested in her. They seemed to accept her interests in art and music, even if they didn't share them. These girls were obviously misunderstood. Her classmates didn't know them that well.

Heather interrupted the conversation to ask for Becky's cell phone number. Overcome by all the attention from her new friends, Becky blanked out and couldn't remember her phone number. She heard laughter from one of the underclassmen sitting within earshot.

"Something funny?" Jeff asked with a look of *how dare you presume to listen to us.*

"Um, no. Sorry," the underclassman sheepishly replied.

"I know what you mean, Becky," Jeff added. "I can't remember mine half the time."

How sweet, Becky thought. Jeff had rescued her from an awkward situation. It was further confirmation for her that there was more to him than he was given credit for.

"Why don't I give you my number. And then just text me, so I'll have your number," Heather told Becky.

Heather stood to leave the group for the night. She hugged everyone.

"It was so nice talking with you. Come sit with us at lunch tomorrow," she said upon reaching Becky.

"Sure, I'd like that," Becky found herself saying with more eagerness than she intended.

Becky lingered for a bit longer before excusing herself. She found herself wishing that she had left with Heather. On her way to her car, Becky noticed Heather's car—a blue Lexus SUV, which was impossible to miss. Becky thought it odd that Heather's car would still be in the youth center parking lot, but she was so overjoyed by her encounters that night that she quickly forgot about it. I've been accepted by the group everyone wants to belong to, she thought.

Shortly after Becky left, Jeff headed toward the back entrance of the youth center. Instead of making his way home, he headed downstairs to the basement. Inside a closet in the back of one of the meeting rooms waited a smiling Heather. "I thought you forgot about me," she said.

"What did you think of her?" Jeff asked.

"I'll work on her. Right now, you have me. Remember?" Heather added.

"Let me know how things proceed," Jeff responded.

"Nothing is going to proceed if you don't quit talking about her," Heather responded.

Jeff smiled before turning off the closet light.

That weekend, Heather took Becky shopping. Heather's family was quite affluent, and she could essentially shop for whatever she wanted. As a homeschooler, Becky had never given much thought about clothes and makeup. They weren't much of a social requirement. It surprised her (and her father) just how much money was required to blend in with the more popular girls.

As they entered one clothing store, Heather quickly snatched up various items from around the store. Becky nervously selected a top from the sale rack. "Try these on," suggested Heather.

Becky was about to explain her budget limitations. But Heather seemed to be already aware of them.

"I can't afford to shop here either, but we both can, using this," Heather said as she waved her father's credit card.

"Your parents don't mind?" Becky asked with an embarrassed look.

"No, honestly. Daddy is a true Texan. Spending money makes him happy, especially when it's spent on his daughters and their friends," Heather added with a reassuring smile.

Heather went on to treat Becky to a shopping spree of makeup and hair products. She went with Becky to have her hair lightened, and the two went together to the tanning salon.

Becky quickly became Heather's new best friend forever. They were together at lunch, after school, and on weekends. The two began to appear frequently on Heather's social media pages. Becky's father was happy that his daughter was not only blending in well but finding acceptance with the more popular students.

Darren pretended not to notice the lavish amounts of money being spent on his daughter. It seemed to make her happy. That was enough for him. Although his happiness for her could not erase his feelings of inadequacy. He wanted the income to provide her with all she wanted. Yet with a modest number of clients, he couldn't hope to match the income of the families of Becky's new friends. He wanted to change that, but he needed help.

Heather invited Becky to a party and afterward to spend the night at Heather's. Becky's father heartily approved of the idea. Becky herself was a bit apprehensive. She had known Heather and her friends for over two months now, but this was the first time she had been invited to a party.

The evening of the party, Heather sent her a text on what to wear. She went through her new clothes and found what she thought Heather meant for her to wear to the party. She slipped the pants on, then looked at herself in the mirror. They fit considerably snug. She felt awkward. She packed the pants and put on her homeschool pants, then went down to meet Heather.

"You're not wearing that?" Heather asked.

"No, I thought my Dad might object to those pants, so I put on something he's used to seeing me in," Becky responded.

Heather smiled and nodded as if she had faced a similar situation with her father. But she knew her father would neither notice nor care what she wore.

They stopped by Heather's house so Becky could change. Before getting ready herself, Heather helped Becky with her hair and makeup, applying considerably more than Becky was used to wearing.

As Heather finished helping her, Becky noticed a small picture of Jeff in a heart-shaped frame beside the bed. It was unclear to Becky that Jeff regarded Heather as more than just a friend; Heather apparently thought otherwise.

Jeff drove Heather's SUV to the party with Heather in front, and Becky, Tad, and Matt in back. The party was at Nicole's house. Her parents were out of town for the weekend.

As they drove up, Becky could see cars occupying the large circular driveway. Jeff parked the SUV on the grass, joining a number of cars already there. Becky could hear loud music emanating from the house. There were throngs of people milling about outside. Jeff yelled greetings to some and exchanged high-fives with others as the group went inside.

Once inside, Heather quickly located Nicole and Lisa in the kitchen. They exchanged hugs and then hugged Becky. There was quite a crowd, Becky noticed. She took it all in. She had never seen a kitchen so large.

The kitchen overlooked an enormous great room, which was adjoined to a huge sunroom. People were laughing, talking, and yelling all throughout the great room. The sunroom appeared to serve as a dance floor.

Becky sat with Heather and the other girls at the kitchen counter facing out towards the great room. Jeff, Tad, and Matt sat or stood nearby.

"What can I get you to drink, ladies?" Jeff asked Becky and Heather as he motioned toward a table, set up as a make-shift wet bar along the wall in the great room.

"Just a Coke for me," Heather responded.

"Just Coke?" Jeff asked with a grin.

"Um, yeah. Just Coke," Heather answered with daggers.

Becky indicated she wanted a Coke as well, and Jeff was off. Becky glanced over at the drink table. There didn't appear to be anything alcoholic available. Was Jeff merely attempting a joke? He quickly returned with the drinks. Becky sipped hers with some hesitancy. She convinced herself it tasted normal.

It was then people began to hit the dance floor. Heather suggested they all dance.

"Why don't you two start things off for us," Jeff answered.

As she and Heather made their way to the dance floor, it occurred to Becky that this was her first attempt to dance.

"I have no idea what I'm doing," Becky said to Heather as the music started.

"Oh, don't worry. No one else does either, as you can see," Heather said with a laugh.

As Becky started to dance, she began to enjoy herself. She began to feel a calm release. It was silly of her to worry about what might have been in her drink.

Jeff sat transfixed with his eyes on Becky.

"You've really got the 'hots' for her there, dude," Tad said to Jeff.

"Yeah, I guess being the gentleman I am, I shouldn't stare," Jeff answered with a grin.

There was at that moment a break in the music. Becky paused to catch her breath and glanced over at the drink table. Heather glanced at Jeff. He and the other boys were momentarily occupied. Samantha Fox just walked in wearing a black dress and heels. Heather glared in her direction.

Samantha walked past the boys on her way to the kitchen. She was a childhood friend of Nicole's. They were still friends, but couldn't spend as much time together as they liked, given Samantha's work schedule.

Although only 17, and still in high school, Samantha worked two jobs to help support herself and her mother. Her father had committed suicide when she was a child. Through a series of temporary jobs and loans from family members, her mother managed to hold the family finances together.

Shortly before Samantha turned 16, her mother was ready to use their house as collateral for a loan from a cousin, who was also a pastor. Before urging Samantha's mother to sign a contract, he prayed with her to "make the right decision, and to be a good steward of the resources she had." Samantha read the contract over and urged her mother not to sign. She correctly perceived that the agreement was little more than a ploy to get the house. Her mother sided with Samantha, which led to her and Samantha both having to endure a long sermon about stewardship from their pastor relative. The episode left Samantha with a lack of trust in pastors. She stopped going to church, much to the chagrin of her mother.

After she turned 16, Samantha began working at The Footbridge—the priciest restaurant in town. She started first as a hostess but quickly became bored by it. She asked the manager if she could help with the bookkeeping. He agreed to give her a try. It quickly became apparent to him that Samantha could finish what he could do in half the time. He promoted her to assistant manager in charge of bookkeeping and inventory and merely helping out as a hostess. Her manager also referred Samantha to a friend who managed a food warehouse, which served most of the chain eateries in the area. Samantha worked one night a week there and as a consultant online as needed.

Samantha would occasionally date, always on her schedule, but she steadfastly refused to date older guys. Still a few older guys persisted. Samantha told them if they wanted to help her, they could buy something for her mother. Hence, her mother ended up with an endless supply of gift cards to the point where she would say, "Sweetheart, I just don't know what I'm going to do with all these cards."

Her manager helped her as well by sharing her story with a few businessmen in town. He hit a nerve of outrage. Before long, Samantha and her mother had free dental care, carpentry work, a new refrigerator, a car and a Jeep, and could have their hair and nails done at no cost.

Things were going well for Samantha, except the one person she wanted in her life as more than a date and a friend was either too busy for her or seemed to view her as a sister. She had known Alex and his family since childhood. She was in love with him. He was the one person she would be willing to make room for in her busy young life.

As she had time, she would stop by Alex's computer lab downtown, much to the delight of his co-workers—an assortment of high-school-age computer and comic book enthusiasts. They viewed Samantha as a kind of goddess and would urge Alex to pursue her. He would always say he feared ruining their friendship, and he didn't know if he could handle her.

"Dude, why don't you at least try? That way we can all live vicariously through you," one co-worker said with exasperation.

On another occasion, a co-worker of Alex's presented Samantha with a book of comic book sketches. These presented Samantha in her black dress and heels as an undercover crime fighter with an assortment of gadgets strapped under her dress. Samantha loved it.

"Thank you, that's so sweet," she said.

Alex happened to be out of the computer lab when Samantha received her comic book sketches. He asked his co-worker who drew the sketches if she liked them.

"Oh yeah, she did. And don't think I'm ever going to wash my face again. She kissed me on the cheek," he said with a jokingly dazed look.

When Alex met Becky, though, his co-workers all knew it was her he wanted. But yet he wouldn't go for her. When Becky started palling around with Heather and sitting on the sinner's side, one of his co-workers lamented, "It's too late, dude. She's gone over to the dark side. You had your chance."

Another co-worker reacted to Alex's dithering by calling him over to his workstation one day.

"Hey Alex, I'm working on a short story. Care to take a look at my working title?" he said.

Alex sensed he was the object of an impending joke, but walked over anyway. He burst out laughing. In bold letters in the middle of a page, he read "Alex: Portrait of an Emasculated Young Man."

Back at the party, as she moved off of the dance floor, Becky noticed the guy at the drink table reaching under the table, grabbing a bottle, and adding some of its contents to ice in a cup before filling the cup with soda. Becky gasped and looked around hurriedly at Heather, but she was preoccupied with Samantha's entrance.

Samantha entered the kitchen knowing full well she was being scrutinized. She found Nicole in the kitchen. Then in mock imitation of Heather, Samantha gave Nicole a series of exaggerated hugs, punctuated by a mauling of her neck. Nicole laughed hysterically while Heather seethed. Jeff let out a catcall. He was ignored and let out another. Unaccustomed to female indifference, Jeff offered a third catcall, this time accompanied by a standing ovation. Samantha slowly turned her head and looked directly at Jeff and mouthed an obscenity. Nicole turned away and feigned a sneeze in order to suppress her laughter. Jeff thrust his chest out and straightened his neck in outrage. Samantha aped his body movements, causing Nicole to double over in a fit of hysterics. Heather put her hands on Jeff's shoulders, urging him to sit down. She glared at Samantha and Samantha glared back.

"Please stop, Samantha. My stomach is going to be sore," Nicole said with carry-over laughter.

"I can't help myself. They're just not used to anyone standing up to them, so it's fun to get their goat," Samantha answered with a smirk of triumph.

"Well, you certainly managed that," Nicole answered still recovering from Samantha's antics.

Samantha then noticed Becky return to her seat next to Heather.

"I don't think I know her," Samantha said, looking at Becky.

"That's Becky. She's new this year. You've probably seen her at school. And you would see her at church if you would go once in a while," Nicole responded.

"Hush, you sound like my mother. So, Becky's hanging out with Heather?" Samantha asked with a pained look.

"Yeah, I think Jeff likes her, so Nicole befriended her for that reason. But she's sweet. She's been hanging out with me some too," Nicole answered.

Samantha sized up the situation. She looked at Becky, then looked at Jeff and Heather, before noticing Matt and Tad.

"Is Becky staying here tonight?" Samantha asked.

"No, I think Becky is staying at Heather's," Nicole responded with a why-do-you-ask look.

"I'm going to go over to talk with my friend Matt," Samantha said.

"I'm your only friend here. Remember. Behave yourself," Nicole said with a nervous smile.

As Samantha approached the group, she received confirmation of what she suspected. Becky looked worried, and looked very pretty, easily more so than Heather. Jeff still looked mad while Matt and Tad looked bored.

As Samantha made her way towards Matt, Jeff stuck out his leg to impede her progress.

"You better watch it, girl," he said with a distinctly unfriendly look.

"Girl? Actually, my full name is Samantha, if you can put that many syllables together."

Jeff shook his head and exhaled as if he had never been so rudely treated. Heather comforted him.

"I don't think we have a seat for you, Samantha," Heather said with a look of disdain.

"Oh, my friend Matt has saved me a seat. Thank you anyway, Heather," Samantha said while settling herself on Matt's lap.

Becky looked at Samantha in amazement. She couldn't believe anyone could openly one-up Jeff and Heather. She momentarily forgot her worries about the party.

"So, are you having a good time, Matt?" Samantha said with a fake smile for Matt, followed by a genuine one for Becky.

"Oh, things just got a lot more interesting for me," Matt responded with a giggle.

At that moment, the boy from the drink table appeared.

"You forgot your Coke," he said to Becky while extending a drink to her.

Becky was once again worried, and couldn't disguise it. She stared at the drink. Samantha intervened. She grabbed the cup and took a sip.

"That's funny. This is Coke and vodka. Bring her back a Coke," she said loud enough for the entire group to hear.

Jeff again looked furious. Heather, Matt, Tad, and the boy from the drink table all looked guilty.

Becky smiled at Samantha, before adding, "Thank you, I would've just started drinking it."

"I'm glad to help. I don't think we've officially met. I'm Samantha," she said while extending her hand to Becky. "Stop by the Footbridge. The Cokes are on me. And come to think of it, we could use a hostess. Really, stop by if you're interested," Samantha said with unusual warmth.

"Thank you so much. I will. I've thought about looking for a job, but I just haven't gotten around to it," Becky said with appreciation.

Samantha smiled at Becky, then she looked at Matt and went back into acting mode.

"So, what do you boys have planned for the evening?" she said with a glance toward Becky while snuggling in closer to Matt.

"Well, I don't know. Guess we'll just hang out here," Matt responded.

"That's all?" Samantha asked, leaning closer to Matt.

"Um, well. Jeff said something about heading up to the lake. Care to join us?" Matt asked.

Heather couldn't hear what was being said, but Samantha made her nervous. Who invited her? She was ruining the evening.

"Looks like you two need to go upstairs and get a room," Heather said, leaning over Becky towards Samantha and Matt.

Samantha put her hand over her heart and slumped over, as if Heather's words had mortally wounded her. Becky suppressed a smile. Samantha leaned in and cupped her hand around Matt's ear and said, "Or instead of going upstairs, we could head over to the church activity center and use one of the downstairs closets."

Matt could not restrain his merriment. And he had a laugh that was loud and deadly, especially for those on the receiving end of it. Heather was furious, knowing the joke was on her.

Jeff stood up. He had enough. "It's time we took this party elsewhere. Shall we?" he said to the group.

Heather looked relieved while Becky looked worried. Matt looked disappointed, knowing Samantha was soon leaving his lap.

"Stop by the restaurant. I'm there most days," Samantha said to Becky while trying to convey reassurance.

"Thank you. I definitely will. And thanks again for letting me know about the job possibility," Becky responded, wishing she had Samantha's confidence.

Samantha stood up to leave. "Don't I even get a goodbye kiss?" Matt asked.

"Sure, I almost forgot," Samantha said while giving him a kick in the shin.

Matt grabbed his leg in pain. "He's such a wuss," Samantha said to Becky with a smile.

Becky watched Samantha wave toward Nicole as she headed out the door. She wished she was going with her. Why had she gotten herself into this?

"I'm going to grab some supplies for the road," Jeff said as he headed toward the drink table.

"You'll have to ignore Samantha. She's only here because Nicole takes pity on her. She's not well liked, as you can tell," Heather said to Becky.

Becky offered Heather a neutral look. She couldn't agree. Though she had just met Samantha, she already liked her and trusted her. She was now unsure of Heather's motives towards her.

Samantha headed home, talked with her mother a little, and then checked her email before getting ready for bed. But she couldn't relax. As much as she tried to rationalize that Becky had willingly gotten herself into the situation she was now in, she still felt a nagging sense of guilt. It was no use trying to sleep. She had to do something. She slipped on her jeans, boots, and sweater. She paused for a moment, strapped on her ankle holster, and reached in the drawer for a gun. On the other ankle, she strapped on her knife sleeve and grabbed a knife. At a party, Jeff would never physically challenge her. By the lake at night with no one around, he would have no hesitation in doing so.

Heather drove the group to the lake. Jeff was drinking heavily and talking loudly, and tossing threatening curses at Samantha.

"She's going to get what's coming to her one of these days. I've had about all of her I can take," he said.

Becky sat quietly and nervously in the back between Tad and Matt, who were both drinking, though not as heavily as Jeff. She had twice suggested to Heather that the two of them should go back to her place. She had been rebuffed both times. Heather seemed to want to assuage Jeff's ego. She was giving him free reign to vent and lead them wherever he wanted.

"You fellas behaving yourselves back there?" Jeff turned to yell at Tad and Matt.

"Well, we're trying to," Tad said while grabbing Becky's thigh.

Becky grabbed his hand and glared at him. Tad put both hands in the air with a look of mock innocence. "I understand, no means no," he said with a laugh.

For his part, Matt had mixed feelings about the evening. He enjoyed trying to talk girls into bed, but if they were unwilling, he was unwilling. He sensed loud and clear that Becky was unwilling, but with equal clarity that her unwillingness mattered little to Jeff. He was in a quandary. Playing football and being a part of the school social scene with all its benefits was his life. If he challenged Jeff, he would be excluded from the group. Jeff owned the school and did what he wanted around town with nary a word of rebuke from the police, coaches, town ministers, or school officials. Ironically, Samantha was the only person who put Jeff in his place. And for that, he respected her, even though he knew she didn't respect him.

Matt was lost in these thoughts as Heather headed down the road leading to the lake.

Samantha checked to see that her mother was asleep, and then quietly walked toward the kitchen for her keys. She entered the garage, went out into the driveway, and then got into her Jeep. She tried not to use the brake, but she gave in a few times for other drivers.

Samantha arrived at the lake turn-off just as Heather was leaving with Jeff, Tad, and Matt. She thought she recognized Heather's SUV, but couldn't be sure. She decided to drive on. At the entrance to the lake, the road forked with a sign pointing left to the campground side and right to the rock wall side. Knowing the rock wall side was officially closed after dark, she turned left. In the campground parking lot, she spotted Alex's truck. She had forgotten he camped out here sometimes. She parked next to him, thinking she could find him and take him with her, and they could go together to the rock wall side.

She reached into her Jeep for a flashlight. She went into the woods. Whew, it was dark, even with the flashlight. She called out for Alex. No answer. She found his campsite. He wasn't there. Did they do something to him, she thought? From a distance, she could see the light of a fire. That was the rock wall side. She walked quickly to that side, glancing around her all the while. She made it to the end of the woods and emerged to see Alex, Becky, and Rex.

Rex barked and growled, but then started wagging his tail. Alex and Becky looked up to see Samantha coming towards them down the hill. They both felt relieved.

Samantha sensed something terrible had happened, but she didn't ask. She knelt down and hugged Becky and looked at Alex with tears in her eyes.

"I'm so sorry. You should have come home with me," Samantha said looking over Becky's shoulder at Alex.

Becky cried with Samantha. Rex licked Becky's hand, then Samantha's. They both tried to stop crying while they petted him.

"Before we go (and we'd better leave now) we have to decide what to do about this," Alex said holding up the cell phone Tad had left behind.

Samantha looked confused. Becky looked once again worried.

"Samantha, they took a video of what they did to Becky—and what they tried to do, using Tad's phone," Alex explained.

"They videotaped it? Wow, that's a new low, even for them. Take the phone by all means. We'll take it to the police. But you're right. We'd better get out of here. They might be back once they realize they've left the phone behind," Samantha answered.

"My dad is away on a WorldEx trip. Let's all go back to my house," Alex answered looking up the hill from whence he came.

Alex slipped Tad's phone into his pocket. They both comforted Becky once more, before helping her up the hill. Once they reached the edge of the woods, they all held hands, and let Rex led them back to Alex's campsite. They packed up Alex's tent and camp gear and headed back to his truck. Becky rode with Samantha. Alex wanted Rex to ride with him, but he hopped in the back of Samantha's Jeep as soon as Becky climbed into it.

As she drove her the boys back into down, Heather still had no idea what happened. She had gotten into a shouting match with Jeff in the parking lot before they left the lake. Why did she have to leave Becky? What happened? And how did Alex happen to show up out of the blue?

The boys, especially Jeff, were way too drunk to offer her an explanation. Heather dropped Matt off. Then, she drove to Jeff's house. Tad couldn't go home this visibly intoxicated. He planned to sober up at Jeff's house, and head home in the morning. Jeff's parents were in bed, but they weren't particularly aware of his whereabouts or activities.

The two headed down to the basement in Jeff's house, and Jeff went to the bathroom to throw up. He came out of the bathroom popping a few aspirins. He handed some aspirin to Tad, before adding, "Dude, let's crash. My head hurts. I don't feel like it now, but tomorrow let's see the video we got tonight."

Tad agreed they needed to get some sleep. Mention of the video momentarily sobered him up. Once Jeff went to his room, Tad reached into his pocket for his phone. It wasn't there. He panicked, removing nearly all his clothes and turning his pockets inside out. He didn't have it. He thought back to when they left the lake in a hurry. They had left without it. That meant evidence of their actions was now out of their hands. Tad sunk his head into the couch. A wave of nausea and regret came over him as he tried to sleep.

CHAPTER 7

Heather sat on her bed furiously calling and then texting Becky. No response. She nervously paced her room. Then, after an agonizing fifteen minutes, Becky responded to one of her many texts. "I'm okay now. I'll get my things from you tomorrow," Becky wrote.

Heather thought of a thousand questions in response to Becky's text. Since Becky ignored all of her previous inquiries about what happened last night, Heather responded with, "Great to know you're okay. There's a party at Lisa's tonight. It's her birthday. Promise it won't be like tonight. Call me."

Sitting on one of the enormous sofas in the great room at Alex's house, Samantha read Heather's message with Becky.

"Oh, so she's going to invite you to another party as if everything's great and wonderful," Samantha said with mounting fury, despite the late hour.

Becky tried to put things in the best light. "Well, maybe, do you think she doesn't know what happened?" Becky asked, looking at both Samantha and Alex.

"It's possible. She has to suspect something major, though," Alex responded.

Samantha exhaled, then clenched her teeth.

"I get it. She dumps you with three drunk football players by the lake after dark, and she wonders what happened," Samantha said with eyes wide open.

"My thoughts exactly," Alex interjected. "But maybe she thought that they wouldn't do (or try to do) what they did."

"I'll go by Nicole's tomorrow and get your things. You weren't planning on going to the party at Lisa's?" Samantha asked Becky.

"Oh, no. That was my last high school party unless I go to one with you two," Becky answered.

Both Samantha and Alex smiled. They were both glad that they seemed to have Becky's trust. They had only been together a short time, but a lasting bond was being formed between them.

"It's been a long night. Let's get some sleep. We'll decide what to do next in the morning," Alex said, standing at the end of the coffee table between the two great room sofas.

"How about if we all sleep out here. I'll take this sofa, and you take the other, Becky. Alex, you grab a sleeping bag and take the floor with Rex," Samantha said with a grin.

"Well, that doesn't sound like a good deal for us guys, but I guess we'll go along with it," Alex said while looking down at Rex with a smile.

Before reclining on the couch, Samantha removed her boots. When doing so, she exposed her gun and knife in her boots for Becky and Alex to see. Becky laughed for the first time that evening.

"Samantha, you're the gal who truly lives up to her comic book character," Alex said as he explained to Becky about the comic book sketches Samantha inspired.

Samantha pointed her chin upward, assuming a thespian pose. Becky again laughed. "Well, I'd better rest up for my next performance," Samantha said with a smirk, as her head hit the pillow.

Alex returned with a sleeping bag and pillow and settled in at the end of the table between the two couches. He looked at Samantha, then Becky. If his friends in the computer lab could only see him now, he thought. They would have to take back everything they said about his manhood.

Becky smiled at Alex and Samantha and stretched out on the sofa. She was inwardly relieved. She thought she could sleep now, knowing they were all here together. As she faded off to sleep, she looked down to see Rex snug against the couch on her side facing the front door.

Samantha woke up first just after sunrise. She started some coffee, and let Rex out in the backyard. She sat in a chair on the sun porch and looked out on the backyard. She thought of how many times she had been in that yard and in the house. Alex and his family had been such good friends to her over the years. They had been kind to her mother as well. They were one of the only families in the church who didn't somehow blame her mother for her father's suicide. Most reacted with cold indifference or somehow insinuated that her mother missed her father's warning signs. It was because of the understanding faith of Alex's family that Samantha thought she might recover her faith someday.

Samantha looked back at Becky and Alex. She knew she had lost Alex to Becky. She could tell by the way he looked at her. It was a look far more significant than any Alex had ever given her. She was ready to give him up and was glad to do it, for he had found someone worthy of his affection.

Besides that, Becky needed her help, not her petty jealousy. She would seek justice for her for what happened, not only for Alex but for Becky herself. She could genuinely see her as a friend, and she had few friends, especially girls.

Samantha turned to see Becky getting up and looking her way. Samantha motioned her towards the sunroom.

"Pull up a chair. Want some coffee? I'll get it. I'm sure there's something in there to eat too," Samantha said.

Samantha returned with coffee and breakfast bars.

"I found these. I guess they're still good. Never know with two bachelors in a house. Or should I say three?" Samantha said as she let Rex in the back door.

Rex sat next to Becky. "I think somebody has a new friend," Samantha said.

"He was your friend first," Becky said smiling while petting Rex.

"No, I've been replaced. It's okay, though," Samantha said with a pout.

"So you've known Alex for a while?" Becky asked Samantha.

"Yes, Alex has been a great friend. Really, his whole family has been a friend to mine," Samantha responded, masking her awkwardness at the question.

"He seems like such a nice guy. I don't know what I would have done if he (and you) hadn't shown up last night," Becky said.

"Alex would have done the same thing for anyone. He's just that way," Samantha responded.

They both turned to see Alex sitting up on the floor. They motioned for him to come into the sunroom.

"Well, look who's up," Samantha said.

"Is that all you two found to eat? There's other stuff in there. I could make some pancakes for us or something," Alex said while still coming awake.

"He's never offered me pancakes," Samantha said with a look of faux amazement.

"That's because you're a superhero. You can live on breakfast bars, unlike ordinary humanity," Alex said with a grin at Samantha and Becky.

As they finished breakfast, Samantha addressed the undesirable. "Well, I wish our being together like this could have occurred under different circumstances, but we're here because of what happened last night. There's a video on Tad's phone?" Samantha asked Alex.

Alex nodded, before adding, "You're right. We need to think about what to do. I'll go with Becky to the police station, and we'll both explain what happened. Then, we'll leave the video with them. If the video captures what I saw, then that should be enough for the police. They'll have to do something," Alex said looking at Becky and Samantha.

"Shouldn't we confirm what's on the video and maybe make a copy of it before turning it over to the police?" Becky asked them both with a determined look.

Samantha was surprised. That's what she would do in the same situation, but she didn't expect it from Becky. After thinking it over a second, Samantha suggested that she would watch the video, and confirm what was captured. Then, Alex could make a copy of it. They all agreed.

Alone, Samantha sat in Alex's room and watched the video. It was far more brutal than she thought. She didn't think anything could shock her. This did. It not only confirmed what Becky described but went well beyond it. Worst of all were the sounds captured. Becky's scream was like something out of a horror movie.

The video also confirmed Alex's version of events. Things transpired not only as he said, but if anything Alex had downplayed his role. Had he not been there and intervened when he did with Rex, things could well have turned out otherwise, and not for the better.

Samantha finished the video and stared blankly at the wall. She was at a loss. What she saw was violent in the extreme. What motivated these guys to videotape themselves was worse. It wasn't enough for them to brutalize a woman, they had to videotape themselves in the act with apparent intent to watch themselves. It was a complete disregard for humanity.

Samantha returned to the sunroom, slowly shaking her head.

"The video didn't show anything?" Alex asked, misinterpreting her body language.

"Oh, yes. Trust me. It's all there. Honestly, I'm shocked. The police will have to do something after watching that," Samantha answered recovering herself.

"Thank you for watching it for me," Becky said to Samantha.

Samantha hugged her. "Don't thank me, thank this guy," Samantha said as she backhanded Alex in the chest.

Alex stuck out his chest in a heroic pose, before adding, "And don't forget the real hero," he said while reaching down to pet Rex.

They all reached down to pet him, while Samantha added, "Rex, you have a lifetime supply of restaurant beef."

Alex had a thought. He hated to broach the subject, but he wanted Samantha's input before going to the police. "I have a thought. Just a thought. We all know how important the football program is to Middleville. Also, I know all three of these guys have been part of the public face (if you will) of Brother Davis's anti-bullying program. Even with this video, I still wonder if they'll get any jail time."

Becky looked dejected. Samantha nodded as if she hadn't thought of that before adding, "Football is important around here, but it shouldn't be that important. I've seen the billboards, and I noticed Matt's t-shirt last night at the party, but why would that be such a big deal?" she said, referring to the anti-bullying program.

"It's become a big deal, not only here, but in churches across the country. And for some reason, Middleville and Brother Davis have taken center stage. But Jeff, Tad, and Matt are part of it. They're on the billboards, mentioned in the articles, and even volunteered as youth counselors, although I'm not sure they do anything except hang out," Alex explained.

"Yeah, reading about the anti-bullying program was one reason my Dad wanted us to move here," Becky added.

"I had no idea. By not going to church, I seem to be clueless about what's going on around here. I'm trying to handle the disconnect between guys volunteering as counselors in this program and what I just saw them do to Becky on video," Samantha said with exasperation.

"It's mind-boggling to me too," Alex added. "The police chief I know from church, but more so from being involved in the community software project. I can't see him looking the other way after seeing the video. I only mentioned this because we have to be aware of it, and be prepared in case nothing happens."

"I'm glad you mentioned it, Alex," Becky said. "I wouldn't have thought of it that way."

"I'm glad you brought it up too. Make a copy of the video, then take the phone to the police. If after talking to the police, it looks like they're not going to do anything, then we'll have to find a way to show the video to someone else," Samantha instructed.

They all agreed with Samantha's plan. Alex made a copy of the video. After lingering a bit longer, they all said goodbye to Rex. Alex left him with plenty of food and blankets in his dog house in the backyard. And they all headed out. Samantha went home to shower and change for work, leaving instructions for them to meet at the restaurant as soon as they left the police station. Alex and Becky drove downtown to the police station, hoping to get there soon after Chief Weston arrived.

Alex and Becky walked into the police station. He was used to going there and was greeted warmly as he walked to the front desk. Becky was greeted with equal warmth, but with an accompanying why-are-you-here look.

"Is Chief Weston in?" Alex asked.

"No he isn't, but he should be here shortly. Anything I can help you with, my friend?" said the officer at the desk.

Alex hesitated for a moment. He didn't want to share this story, and especially the video, with anyone else but Chief Weston.

"We'll just wait here until he arrives. Thank you," Alex said as he motioned towards a waiting area.

The officer nodded. He then offered Alex and Becky some doughnuts and coffee. They both politely declined.

They waited for what seemed like forever, but it was less than ten minutes. The chief arrived through the side door. He grabbed a doughnut and coffee as he made his way around to the front desk. The chief noticed Alex first. He nodded, but then his face registered surprise at seeing Becky. The chief approached them.

"Looks like everything's all set for the banquet tonight. As always, we appreciate your help. Looks like you've got your body-guard there with you," Chief Weston said as he smiled at Becky.

Alex smiled and introduced Becky. With everything that had happened, he had forgotten about the banquet tonight at the school gym. The theme of the banquet was "Partners in Crime Prevention," with police, school, and church officials as well as parents and students, all planning to be present. Alex's social media monitoring software and the anti-bullying program were two of the speaking topics. Alex had planned to make an appearance at the banquet to check the audio and video setup, but his co-workers in the computer lab were supposed to have the audio and video setup in place.

"I'm glad to help out with the banquet," Alex said. "But that's not why we're here. Could we talk with you in private?" Alex said, looking from Becky to the chief's concerned face.

"You bet. Let's go back to my office," the chief said as he led the way.

Chief Weston settled in behind his desk on which rested a Bible and pictures of his wife and daughters. The wall behind him contained an assortment of community awards and photos. In only one was the chief wearing a smile, and that was a photo of him shaking hands with a smiling Brother Davis.

An officer approached the chief's office door with a question about an administrative matter. The chief answered, and then instructed the officer to shut the door.

"How can I help you?" the chief said looking from Alex to Becky.

"I'm not sure how to start, chief," Alex began. "We're here to report an assault. Well, an attempted rape."

The chief raised his eyebrows and reached into his desk drawer for a legal pad. "Okay. Tell me what happened," he said as he reached for a pen.

Alex started off by explaining that he had gone to the lake to camp and take photos, but then he heard voices and what he thought were screams from the rock wall side of the lake. The chief listened. Alex and Becky tried to read his face. At the mention of the names of the three football players, the chief exhaled and rubbed his mustache.

Alex went on to explain every detail of what occurred but omitted any mention of the video.

After Alex finished, the chief quickly looked over his notes. "I want to thank you both for coming in. You did the right thing. In this situation, though, Alex, it was okay to get your dog after them, but shooting arrows like you did is not. Someone could have gotten hurt, and then you'd have been at fault. I'll look over your version of events, and then I'll question the boys about what they think happened. This happened at night, and there was alcohol involved, so it might be easy to misread someone's intentions," the chief said with a stern look at Alex and then at Becky.

"I can assure you, chief," said Becky with mounting anger, "that I wasn't drunk. And I asked to be taken back to Heather's house. I did have my cell phone with me, and I suppose I could have called my Dad. But I'm not even sure if he would've known how to find me. We're new to the area."

"Even so," said the chief, "you did consent to go the lake. Am I correct?"

"I didn't think going to the lake meant consenting to rape. I thought the boys were going to drink, but I didn't think they would try what they did," said a visibly angry Becky.

Alex went on to reiterate that he witnessed everything through night vision goggles, so he saw what happened. He went on to defend his use of the bow, explaining that he had never gotten Rex after anyone before and that he was a family dog. Finally, Alex mentioned the video.

"Chief, there's just one more thing," said Alex, as he reached into his cargo pants pocket for Tad's phone. "On this phone is a video that will confirm what Becky and I have just told you. And I think if we all watch it together..."

The chief put both hands up, and interrupted Alex. "Hold on. Whose phone is this, and how do you have it?"

"It's Tad's phone. He videotaped what they did (and tried to do) to Becky. In the confusion of what happened, he left his phone at the lake when he left with the others," Alex explained.

"Okay, okay. Tell you what, I'll take a look at the phone and the video as part of the investigation. And as I said, I'll talk with the boys and possibly others at the party. I may need you both to come in again to answer more questions. In the meantime, I would ask you both to not discuss this with anyone, since this is now part of a police investigation. But again, I want to thank you both for coming in," said the chief, as he made direct eye contact with Alex and Becky.

When Alex and Becky left his office, the chief exhaled and looked at the cell phone Alex had given him. Officially, it should be filed as evidence, and officially, an investigation of an alleged crime should now be open. But the chief understood well the importance of the football program to Middleville. Additionally, Brother Davis's anti-bullying program had become an integral part not only of civic life locally but nationally, especially within evangelical circles. Families (and even a few businesses) had made the decision to relocate in Middleville based on the notoriety of the program. Jeff, Tad, and Matt were identified with the program. Their names and faces had appeared in promotional literature in connection with it. People in town knew their names. To go after them as part of a public investigation would be a black eye on the community.

The chief was mad at himself. He should have seen this coming. For the past year, he had ignored several complaints about one or more of the boys' behavior around town. There was an incident involving Mr. Simmons in the drug store. There was another incident in which a drunken Jeff threatened the movie theater manager, another in which all three boys knocked over a convenience store owner. And that wasn't the full extent of the complaints. The chief had looked the other way for too long. He made excuses for the boys. They were just letting off steam. He did similar things at their age. He thought by getting the boys involved in church and the anti-bullying program; it would help temper their behavior. But it did little good, as much as he tried to convince himself otherwise.

It made matters worse that the boys' behavior was now impacting Alex, for whom he had the highest regard. Alex's software team had been a genuine help to the department and the community. Lives had probably been saved because of their expertise. Alex was everything the other three boys were not. In fact, the chief had sometimes wished that Alex would take an interest in one of his daughters, both of whom were high school age.

Worst of all, however, was the look on Alex's and Becky's faces as they left. The chief looked as authoritative as he could, but he could tell they knew better. There would be no investigation. This would be handled internally. The chief had no choice, and Alex and Becky knew it.

The chief pulled out a business envelope from his desk and placed Tad's phone in it. He put the phone between two old phone books in his desk drawer and locked it. As he did, there was a knock at the door. A young lieutenant opened the door with a question about the banquet that evening. The chief dutifully answered. The lieutenant followed up his question by suggestively telling the chief that he hadn't seen Alex's girlfriend before.

"Well, now you've seen her! Happy now?" the chief angrily retorted.

"Easy, chief. I didn't mean anything by it," the lieutenant responded.

"Watch yourself, lieutenant. Watch yourself," the chief said.

As the lieutenant closed the door, the chief thought of his next move. Something had to be done, and it couldn't wait. The chief picked up the phone and called Brother Davis.

Becky called her father after leaving the police station to say that she was having lunch with some friends and would be home that afternoon. When asked about the previous evening, she tried to answer as truthfully as possible. Despite her horrible ordeal at the lake, she did very much enjoy getting to know Alex and Samantha. She knew she would have to tell her father about what occurred. She dreaded it, most of all because she thought that he might blame himself. If only they hadn't moved, or if he hadn't been so eager to send her to public school, he might say to himself. Nevertheless, at some point, she would have to tell him.

Samantha had just finished opening the restaurant when Alex and Becky arrived. She was behind the bar working at a laptop as they entered. She looked up quickly. She wanted to hear everything. She showed them to a table in the back.

"Order whatever you like, Becky. Alex has it covered. Really, it's on the house for you both. Give me just a little bit," she said as she called a waiter over to take their orders.

The waiter took their orders, and Samantha soon arrived with Cokes for each of them. Sitting next to Becky, Samantha decided to eat with them.

"Okay, I can't wait any longer. How did it go? What did he say when you showed him the video?" Samantha said, her eyes panning from Alex to Becky.

"He said he would consider it as part of the investigation, but he wouldn't watch it with us. Honestly, I didn't leave there with a good feeling," Alex said, as Samantha's eyes shifted to Becky.

"I didn't either," Becky added. "He seemed to blame Alex and me more than I was comfortable with. He asked me if I willingly went to the lake as if by consenting to go, I consented to everything else."

"He said that to you?" Samantha asked with eyes widened in anger.

"He didn't use those exact words, but that's how it sounded to me," Becky responded, looking at Alex for confirmation.

"I took it that way too," Alex said. "I really felt bad for Becky. The chief also told me I would have been at fault had someone gotten wounded by the arrows. That bothered me. It was like he deflected attention away from the assault on Becky by focusing on how I might have hurt someone y trying to help her."

Becky looked at Alex with the most caring look. Samantha did as well, but then her jaw tightened.

"You were right, Alex," Samantha said. "Football trumps every-thing around here."

"Football does. But it's also now wrapped up with the anti-bully-ing program, which has gone national, as I mentioned this morning. The chief is active in church and in the program," Alex responded.

Samantha exhaled, and then rubbed her forehead. "Okay, here's my idea," she said. "Let's give the chief a week (possibly two). If we don't hear anything, then we have to go to someone else, someone with some influence in town. Mr. Simmons would be my first choice. He eats lunch here a lot during the week, and he knows everyone in town. He's always sweet to me too."

Alex and Becky agreed. Samantha then tried to lighten the mood for them.

"Becky, I take it back, we'll have to take your lunch and Alex's out of your first paycheck. Really, though, I do wish you'd consider the hostess job. If nothing else, it might help take your mind off things."

Becky agreed to start working at the restaurant. Samantha had stopped by Heather's to get Becky's things, which she gave to her. Alex then drove Becky home. He didn't want to leave her side. She didn't want to leave him.

"Thank you seems so trite for everything you've done for me," Becky said as Alex dropped her off. "Call me often."

Alex was delighted to say he would. He walked her to the door. They embraced and parted for the day.

Becky entered the rental house dreading that her father would pump her with questions about the previous evening. But he wasn't home. She read his note on the kitchen table, "Becky, I had to run an errand. There are some Chinese leftovers in the fridge. Help your-self! Love, Dad."

Mr. Darren Worthington, Becky's father, sat across the desk from Brother Davis in his office. Chief Weston sat to Darren's right.

"Mr. Worthington, thank you for coming in on such short notice," Brother Davis began. "I regret we didn't have the opportunity to meet when you first joined the church. As the church has grown larger over the years, I've had to delegate some things, more things than I would care to. Before I go any further, I'll let Chief Weston explain why we're here."

"Mr. Worthington," Chief Weston began to a wide-eyed father, "there was an incident last night out by the lake involving your daughter and three of the young men on the football team. What exactly happened is still unclear. We're still gathering all the facts. I wanted to assure you, though, as police chief, we're investigating the incident."

"I'd like to hear exactly what happened," said Darren.

The chief went on to explain what happened, and how Alex and Becky came to him to report the incident. In so doing, the chief was careful to avoid blaming Becky in any way. Yet he was careful to avoid any suggestion of outright guilt on the part of Jeff, Tad, or Matt. The chief mainly characterized what happened as a possible misunderstanding on Alex's part. He may have overreacted in the dark and mistook horseplay for something far worse. It was still too early to tell.

As soon as the chief finished, Brother Davis interjected, "I'm confident Chief Weston and his staff will conduct a thorough and complete investigation. You can rest assured of that. In the meantime, we want you and Becky to feel welcome in Middleville. I hope you'll allow us to show you how glad we are you're here. The man from whom you rent your house is a member of this church. I've taken the liberty to contact him, and he's agreed to allow you free use of the house for as long as you like. Also, I understand that starting a brokerage business can be challenging for someone new to an area. I've also taken the opportunity to contact two of the more prominent men in our church, and they've agreed to help you grow your business. We want you and Becky to feel at home here, and we hope you'll allow us to help you."

Darren was at a loss. He did, in fact, need the help. His business gave him enough money to pay the bills, but just barely. He had little extra money. Yet Darren knew the generosity now being extended to him was motivated by more than just compassion. It was the equivalent of paying him civil damages for whatever may have happened to Becky.

"I appreciate the generosity," Darren said, putting on his manliest face. "But in accepting it, I don't want whatever happened to be swept under the rug. If these young men harmed my daughter, I want them held responsible."

Brother Davis and Chief Weston both assured Darren they were not interested in sweeping things under the rug, and as fathers, they could understand how he must feel. The chief also told Darren that while he would be open in discussing the progress of the investigation, for Becky's sake, it would be best to maintain confidentiality.

"In this town, people do a lot of talking, more than they should," the chief warned Darren.

As Darren finished meeting with Brother Davis and Chief Weston, Alex was in the computer lab downtown. His co-workers sensed something significant had occurred. Alex seemed alternately giddy and distracted, more so than usual. Alex tried to pass off his mood on his success in capturing some great photos the previous evening, but his friends weren't buying it. Before they could press him too far, though, Alex headed off to the school gym to check on the audio-video setup for the community banquet that evening.

As Alex entered the gym, he noticed only a handful of people had arrived. There were a few people putting the finishing touches on tablecloths and chairs. He noticed the audio-visual team busy on the speaker's platform and headed that way. As he proceeded that way, he encountered the church secretary, Betty McBride.

In her late sixties, Betty had been Brother Davis's secretary for years. Her husband had died tragically in a construction accident nearly twenty-five years ago. She continually held out hope of finding love again, but her hopes were never realized. She would joke about her loneliness as a way of coping with it.

"Hello, Alex," Betty began. "Here to check on things as always? It looks like tonight is going to be some night. Brother Davis must want everything to be perfect. Chief Weston stopped by the office earlier. And Mr. Worthington stopped by also. He seems like such a fine man, and I enjoyed meeting his daughter, Becky. Oh, if only I were younger. But, God may still have someone out there for me. Alex, are you all right?"

"Oh, yes. I'm sorry," Alex responded with a troubled look. "I just remembered something I needed to check on for tonight. It was nice talking with you, Miss Betty."

Alex walked to the speaker's platform to talk with the audio-visual team. He went over a few things with them, but his mind was now elsewhere. Possibly Chief Weston's visit with Brother Davis was related to tonight's program, but there could be only one explanation for Becky's father visiting Brother Davis and Chief Weston: They told Mr. Worthington what happened to his daughter. But why would Brother Davis be involved in the investigation? Alex didn't have an answer.

The "Partners in Crime Prevention" banquet attracted all of official Middleville. Along with Chief Weston and Brother Davis, the school board president, the mayor, and the district attorney were present. Also on hand for the event were coaches and players from Middleville High as well as the school principal and a representative from Alex's software team. Alex had intended to check on the audio-video setup for the evening, but not attend the event. After hearing about the meetings in Brother Davis's office, he decided to watch things from the back of the gym in the audio-video control booth.

A few minutes into the event, Alex noticed Jeff, Tad, and Matt take seats at a table near the front. He had not noticed them before. The evening proceeded with various community awards and speeches. Mayor Lance Collins was the evening's master of ceremonies. He presented Brother Davis with the award for "Community Servant of the Year" for the communitywide (and now nationwide) success of the anti-bullying program.

Known for his long-winded speeches, Mayor Collins heaped high praise on Brother Davis for "his unflappable efforts to unite disparate entities across this community." The mayor also called Davis "a man with a servant's heart" and "a leader who inspires others to follow in his footsteps." According to the mayor, among those Davis had inspired were members of the Middleville High School football team. "As I see young men like Jeff Taylor, Tad Smith, and Matt Nelson, I see the same empathy, compassion, and respect for others I see in Brother Davis," the mayor proudly declared. Brother Davis and Chief Weston shifted uncomfortably in their chairs. Matt looked embarrassed. Jeff and Tad smiled like identity thieves being commended for honesty. Alex was horrified at the remark, but more so that the three were attending a community event as if nothing had happened. He couldn't handle anymore. He left the event.

Becky tried to study, but her mind couldn't rest. Her father had returned from his errand. Rather than greeting her warmly and asking about her evening, he hugged her as if one might hug a returning veteran. Did he know what happened, she wondered? Should she talk with him about it? She needed to talk with Alex and Samantha.

Becky was relieved when Alex called that night. She missed him already. They talked back and forth for a while before Becky explained that she thought her father was not himself towards her. "I think I know the reason," Alex said. "I can't say for sure, but your Dad may know what happened."

Her father's behavior now made sense to her. She and Alex agreed that she should talk with her father about the assault. Yet there never seemed to be a good time to broach the subject. And besides, she rationalized, if he already knows, then why upset him all the more. She knew, however, that this was being unjust to her father.

That evening, everyone seemed to be having a good time at Lisa's birthday party, except for Heather. She knew something had occurred the previous night—something awful. But Jeff and Tad were mum. During a break in the dancing, Heather noticed Matt sitting off to himself.

"Well, is someone feeling anti-social tonight?" she said, as she took a seat next to him.

"Well, I guess you could say that. I still haven't recovered from last night," Matt said trying to force a smile.

"Speaking of last night, what happened? I can't get anything out of Jeff," Heather said.

"Let's just say we had a little too much to drink, and things got out of hand," Matt responded.

"Just how out of hand did things get? Did you guys try what I think you did?" Heather asked.

Matt didn't say anything or react in any way at first.

"Look, we've been told not to talk about what happened, but I think you've figured it out," he said. "I wish I could take back what happened. I'm not proud of it. I'm here tonight because of Lisa. This is my last party. It's just no fun anymore."

"Thank you for confirming what I suspected. At least I know now," Heather said as she walked away.

On the other side of town, Brother Davis sat at his desk in his home office looking over his notes for Sunday's sermon. Before setting to work, he prayed (as he always did) for the Lord's guidance. Yet his prayer felt false. Could a prayer for God's guidance be answered if one ignored the guidance he had already received? Davis wouldn't face this question or its answer. Through slow compromise and without realizing it, he was losing his faith. His ministry was becoming an extension of him and the assertion of his will, not the

Lord's. After several minutes of reading over the same paragraph in his notes, Davis sighed, turned out the light on his desk, and headed to bed for the night.

CHAPTER 8

Scott Thornton sat in his pickup in the parking lot of First Baptist of Middleville on a sunny Saturday morning. He was early. He looked at his phone as he waited for Pastor Crabtree to arrive. He noticed he had a voicemail. Must've missed it, he thought.

Scott played the message. "Scott, this is Pastor Crabtree. I'm so sorry to have to do this at the last minute. My daughter is playing in a softball game this morning, and I forgot I promised her I'd go. You're welcome to come over and join us if you don't have any plans this morning. Talk with you soon, Scott."

Scott tried to suppress feelings of anger. He was a roofer, and he had turned down an opportunity to meet with a prospective customer so he could be available today. Beyond that, he had things to catch up on around the house, as his wife, Jill, had reminded him. Perhaps he was overreacting and should drop by the softball game. Somehow he felt he couldn't, though. His wife was not expecting him home until late that evening. After checking his phone once more, he sighed, and pulled out of the church parking lot, and headed out towards Texas Heritage University.

As he made the drive, Scott thought of everything he had learned in his evangelism training with Pastor Crabtree. Scott and Jill had moved to Middleville within the past year. Jill was eager for Scott to establish his business before becoming involved in church activities. Yet, after a few months, Scott felt established enough in his business to devote more time to church activities.

Scott felt a passion for evangelism and would hold talks with himself about how the church needed to do more to witness to the lost. One day, Jill overheard him talking with himself.

"Honey, who are you talking with?"

"Oh, just me," Scott replied with embarrassment.

"You can talk to me, silly," Jill said, planting a kiss on her husband.

After talking with Scott for some time about his desire to share the Gospel, Jill realized how serious he was.

"Honey, if this is what you want to do, then talk with someone at the church," she said.

With his wife's encouragement, Scott sought out opportunities for evangelism ministry at First Baptist. The church's leadership put Scott in touch with Pastor Crabtree who, in addition to serving as youth minister, was serving as outreach pastor. After meeting with Scott and seeing his passion, Pastor Crabtree decided on a mission trip to nearby Texas Heritage University. The pastor had ministry contacts there. He thought Scott's passion and his skill as an acoustic guitarist would make a winning ministry combination on campus.

Pastor Crabtree and Scott set a date to travel to the university. Scott and his wife were excited. Although the pastor had not detailed precisely what type of ministry activities they would be involved in, Scott was happy to have an opportunity to pursue his passion.

As Scott neared the university that Saturday morning, he stopped to ask directions to the Evangelical Student Union on campus. Pastor Crabtree had mentioned that they would meet with Alvin Lee, a college friend of the pastor, who was director of the Evangelical Student Union. Scott fumbled in the front seat for Alvin's cell phone number. Alvin was unavailable.

Scott pulled into the parking lot of the Evangelical Student Union. As he did, he remembered he had promised Jill he would call her as soon as he arrived on campus. He hesitated to call. She would wonder why he made the trip alone. Jill was unavailable also.

Scott approached the door to the student union with his guitar in hand. The door was locked. He peered inside. There were no signs of life yet. Scott sighed and checked his watch. Maybe he should head home, he thought. But he talked himself out of it. Perhaps he could get some coffee, find a place to play his guitar, and pass out some of the Gospel tracts he had taken along with him. Scott made his way around campus to find a place to get some coffee.

On the other side of campus, Emily Rosenthal checked the clock in her dorm room. It was getting late. She had to get up to meet with a student to tutor that morning at Oneness, a favorite coffee shop for the campus alternative-leaning students.

Emily pulled herself together and began getting ready. She was a strikingly beautiful girl with short, bleached-blonde hair. Despite putting forth minimal effort in the clothes or makeup department, she attracted male attention and female envy wherever she went on campus. She put on her favorite attire—a black turtleneck, skinny jeans, and boots. She grabbed her book bag and phone and left her dorm room to make the walk to the coffee shop.

Scott turned the corner in front of Oneness and noticed a sign outside announcing coffee specials. A few students were milling about outside the coffee shop. Scott parked on a nearby side street and gathered his guitar case and Gospel tracts.

He had not had the opportunity to show his tracts to Pastor Crabtree, but he assumed that the tracts would meet with the pastor's approval. The tracts bore the title, "More Than One Way?" Inside, they shared the uncompromising message of Christ as the one and only way to heaven, not as an option among other religions and philosophies. Before making his way inside Oneness, Scott put his supply of tracts inside his guitar case.

Once inside the coffee shop, Scott's blue-collar looks caught the attention of the shop staff and gathering customers. But his guitar case put them at ease. Perhaps he is one of us after all, they thought. The staff smiled at Scott and his guitar and were more than happy to oblige his requests for a chair and desire to play his guitar in front of Oneness.

As Scott sipped his coffee, he looked at the stack of tracts in his guitar case. He moved his chair close to a nearby newspaper stand and set the tracts on top of the stand next to his coffee. He tuned his guitar. More students began to trickle into Oneness, and they paused to smile at Scott and his guitar. He smiled back and felt comfortable with his decision to be there.

On the other side of campus, Emily made her way slowly toward Oneness. On her way, she encountered an old acquaintance. In addition to being beautiful and brainy, Emily was kind. It was one more thing about her that alternately endeared her to or infuriated others.

Emily spied a student seated alone in the quad, whom she thought she recognized. The student appeared to have tears in her eyes. Emily approached her.

"Hi. Is everything okay?"

The student nodded in the affirmative before sharing with Emily an upsetting story about her doubts about her boyfriend's love for her. Emily listened attentively and empathetically without betraying the slightest bit of impatience. She ignored a text message alert on her phone from the student she planned to tutor.

As Emily continued to talk with the troubled student, Scott was well into another Gospel instrumental on his guitar. He was satisfied with his guitar playing, but more satisfied that he had the opportunity to hand out a fair number of his Gospel tracts to students entering or leaving the coffee shop. Scott looked at his nearly empty coffee cup and decided to make his way inside for a refill. As he did, he gathered a few of his tracts. Maybe he could give some out to customers inside the coffee shop.

As Scott approached the counter to request a refill, he was met with deeply unfriendly looks from the coffee shop staff. Taken aback a bit, he looked behind him to see if the unfriendliness was intended for someone else.

"May we help you?" asked the coffee shop manager.

"Sure, I was hoping I could get a refill," Scott said as he slid his nearly empty cup across the counter.

"I'm afraid we're fresh out of refills, at least for you," the manager said in a steely tone. Scott looked puzzled.

"Is there a problem?" he asked.

"We don't appreciate you being here with, with *this*," the manager said while waving one of the tracts close to Scott's face.

Scott struggled to control his temper, before adding, "Look, I asked you if it was okay."

"Correction," the manager replied, "you asked for a chair and permission to play your guitar in front of the shop. *This* goes against everything we stand for," the manager added with a Gospel tract in his extended hand.

"What do you stand for?" Scott retorted.

The manager became enraged. "Look, I don't have time to argue with some brick-layer preacher or whatever it is you are. You're not welcome here. Get out!"

"It sounds like you could use this," Scott said as he slid a copy of his tract across the counter toward the manager.

With that action, the manager lost all composure. He unleashed a barrage of vile and blasphemous profanity at Scott within earshot of the now half-full coffee shop.

Scott was stunned. He thought he had been around the block, but he had never heard profanity this abusive. He simply threw both hands in front of him, then turned and walked outside the coffee shop. The manager, staff, and some of the customers erupted in applause.

Scott walked over to retrieve his guitar and remaining tracts before heading back to his truck. He half expected his guitar to be damaged. It was still intact, although some of his tracts had been torn to shreds, and now blew about on the sidewalk. Scott considered what he should do. He felt both angry and dejected. He glanced at the storefront next to the coffee shop. A "Now Leasing" sign was in the window. Without quite knowing why, Scott moved near the empty storefront and took out his guitar and remaining tracts.

A small group of coffee shop customers eyed Scott as he tuned his guitar in front of the neighboring store. Scott glanced their way before playing and now singing "Amazing Grace" at the top of his lungs. The manager and staff of Oneness quickly emerged on the sidewalk and began shouting obscenities in Scott's general direction. Scott continued to play and sing with renewed vigor.

* * *

Across campus, Emily had finished consoling the student regarding her boyfriend's love for her and was now making her way to Oneness. On her way, she thought of Halle, the sophomore student she was to meet at the coffee shop. This would be their second tutoring session, but Emily was pleased with the progress they were making. As she drew closer to the coffee shop, she heard loud shouting in the distance. She strained to listen but was still too far away to discern the words.

Emily turned the corner and was now in direct line of sight with the coffee shop. She was startled. Surrounding the storefront neighboring the coffee shop were the shop owner, staff, and other students, most of whom she recognized. The group was standing locked in arms and shouting, "Bigot, go home!"

As Emily moved closer to see what the uproar was about, she spotted Halle locked in arms with the other students. Halle and the other students noticed Emily approaching and motioned for her to join them. Emily moved closer to the group. She spotted and heard a man with a guitar. He played and sang "Amazing Grace" behind the locked arms. Emily moved closer to Halle and leaned in to ask her about their tutoring session. As she did, Halle unlocked her arms from the rest of the group. Scott made momentary eye contact with Emily and thrust a tract into her hand. The protesting students turned angrily and glared at Scott. He resumed playing and singing "Amazing Grace" as loud as he could, while the protesting students began shouting profanity as loud as they could.

"Let's go inside, Miss Emily," Halle yelled over the din of the students.

Feeling quite bewildered, Emily made her way inside the coffee shop with Halle. After getting coffee, they seated themselves away from the window to avoid the distractions outside. As they settled in a booth, they both noticed the flash of police car lights in front of the store.

Outside on the sidewalk, two policemen approached the protesting students.

"Just what is going on here?" Chief Pitts demanded.

The manager of Oneness emerged and handed the policeman one of Scott's Gospel tracts. The Chief quickly took the tract, opened it, and glanced at its contents.

"I'm not seeing a problem here," the chief remarked with a heavy sigh of disgust.

"I'm afraid we do see a problem," the coffee shop manager responded.

"Yeah, we wouldn't want any of you all to end up in church. Not that it would do any of you any good," the chief replied, with a dismissive glance at the gathered throng of students.

The coffee shop manager raised his voice in protest. Chief Pitts held his hand up to indicate silence. As he did, the chief stepped through the group of students.

"Come on, son. Let's get you out of here," he said with a sympathetic glance at Scott.

Inside the coffee shop, Emily continued her tutoring session with Halle, who was reading Orwell's Animal Farm for a literature class.

"Miss Emily, I like it when he says, 'All animals are equal, but some are more equal than others,'" Halle said to Emily.

"That's a great line, honey. Now think about why you like that and write down a few thoughts in your own words," Emily responded.

Like her Southern belle Mother, Emily called virtually everyone (male or female) honey or sweetheart. Halle found it charming, so she reciprocated by calling Emily, "Miss Emily."

As Emily tried to stay focused on tutoring Halle, Chief Pitts escorted Scott out of town to a truck stop along the freeway. There in the parking lot, the policeman apologized to Scott for the rough treatment the students had given him. The policeman offered to buy Scott lunch. He refused and was on his way home to Middleville.

Later that afternoon, Emily sat in her dorm room. She mulled over the events of the morning. She couldn't understand or relate to the students' anger. What were they so afraid of? Was one guy with his guitar and Gospel tracts that much of a threat? Apparently so.

As if remembering, Emily dug into her book bag and retrieved the tract that Scott had given her. She adjusted herself in bed on her elbow and began reading the tract. As she read, she moved to the chair, then stood and continued to read. The tract voiced the evangelical faith of her mother. It was a faith that Emily had never considered for herself. Neither was she inclined to the secular Judaism of her father. She had not considered herself religious or non-religious. As she read, the tract sang to her. It made perfect sense. She felt confused. She felt something deeply lacking in herself that could only be satisfied by the Christ that the tract spoke of. She set the tract down and then noticed on the back of it a suggested prayer. She knelt by her bed and prayed the prayer. She opened her eyes and smiled.

CHAPTER 9

Emily woke up early that Sunday and called her mother. "Mother, it's me. Can I go to church with you today?"

"Why of course, sweetheart. To what do I owe the honor of your presence?" Emily's mother, Carol, replied.

"It's too much to share over the phone. I'll need to borrow a dress though," Emily responded.

Emily shared her newfound faith with her mother. Carol was delighted but dumbstruck. She and her husband Allan had agreed to let Emily find her way. They neither encouraged nor discouraged Emily in matters of faith. Hence, Emily's outlook on religion was (until now) basically secular. Carol had always assumed that if Emily were to ever convert to Christianity, it would be through an intellectual appeal. Yet, Emily had embraced Christian faith by way of the humblest of means.

Carol's church was an independent Presbyterian church with evangelical leanings. The church had split from the mainline Presbyterian church a decade ago. The church membership was affluent enough to write a check to the local Presbytery, so its property would no longer be held in trust for the benefit of all. Emily had been baptized as an infant in the church and would occasionally attend with her mother on holidays.

When Emily and her mother arrived at church that morning, her mother went to her Sunday school class and insisted Emily attend the college class. "Maybe some of your friends will be there, honey," Carol said, as they went to their separate classes.

Emily walked into the college Sunday school class. It had yet to begin, and students were milling about in various places in the room.

"Emily?" said a voice to her immediate right.

Emily turned to greet and hug Judy, a Chinese student whom she had tutored. It was Emily who had suggested to the student that she take the name Judy to make it easier for Americans. "It's so good to see you here," said Judy.

Emily went on to answer the inevitable question of what had brought her to Sunday school. She shared the story of her conversion with Judy. Then Emily pulled from her purse the tract that inspired her conversion. Judy's eyes widened with a mixture of delight and surprise.

"Oh. That is so wonderful! I don't think I've ever seen one of those on campus," Judy added.

About this time a Chinese male appeared behind Judy. She introduced her boyfriend to Emily. He smiled and looked Emily over from head to toe. Judy gave him the daggers, sternly addressed him in Chinese, and then smiled at Emily.

As Judy and her boyfriend took their seats, Emily helped herself to the coffee. As she did, he was once again greeted by a familiar face.

"Emily, I thought that was you," said Amy, a fellow English major.

Her boyfriend, Stan accompanied Amy. Emily soon had a sinking feeling that she would have to explain her presence in church to everyone who recognized her. But she put on her brave Southern belle face and launched into her explanation. As Emily pulled the tract from her purse, Amy frowned and glanced at Stan who suppressed a smirk. "Well, that's great. Why don't you join us?" Amy added with feigned genuineness.

That morning the class was privileged to host Blaine Winthrop, a new intern at the Evangelical Student Union. Blaine was introduced as that morning's guest teacher. The class nodded approvingly as Blaine was introduced, especially as it was revealed that he was involved in student ministry during his undergraduate days at Harvard. Amy glanced at Emily as Blaine took the podium.

Blaine shared how privileged and delighted he was to be there, and how excited he was to begin his ministry on campus. He opened with a self-deprecating joke or two about adapting to Texas life. He then launched into his lesson for the morning.

Blaine's lesson text for the morning was Luke 14:13-14. Emily looked on with Amy to follow along with the Gospel lesson about inviting the poor and the lame to our banquet.

"As we ponder the application of these verses," said Blaine, "I would encourage us to consider two themes. One is that our church should be a church without walls. Two is that we must build bridges with those who cannot repay us."

Emily thought the lesson would emphasize themes of compassion toward the poor and needy. Yet it veered in an unexpected direction.

"Some within our evangelical community (perhaps even on this campus) want to put up walls around our community," Blaine continued. "These misguided individuals want to exclude certain students and faculty from our fellowship. But we as the new generation of evangelicals must reach out to those who cannot repay us, such as members of the gay and lesbian community and the theological universalists. Don't misunderstand, we as a church are not obliged to agree. Theological diversity and doubt are our friends. Our evangelical faith can stand the test to follow truth wherever it leads. We need not isolate a handful of verses to exclude those with whom we disagree. Our God is bigger than such a limited perspective."

During the lesson, Amy and Stan nodded approvingly, while glancing at Emily to gauge her level of agreement. Judy frowned throughout the lesson and glanced at Emily with a troubled look. For her part, Emily was taking it all in, not being sure what to make of what she heard. What she heard sounded like something most students would agree with, even those who wouldn't be caught dead in church. She wondered what the end game was of such a theology. She also wondered what her mother would think of the lesson.

After the lesson, Amy and Stan introduced Emily to Blaine. He gave Emily a look of significance. As Emily left to join her mother for the morning's service, Amy related to Blaine the story of Emily's recent conversion. Blaine listened attentively, wanting to know where and when this happened. He curiously seemed more alarmed than pleased by Emily's conversion being inspired by a tract. But in the end, he added, "Well, I suppose one cannot completely discount old-fashioned approaches."

Over lunch at her parents' house, Emily shared the details of her conversion with her father. He was surprised by the news but wanted nothing more than his daughter's happiness. Allan kissed his daughter on the forehead before smiling at both his wife and Emily.

"Well, it looks like it's one Jew against two evangelicals now. I'm outnumbered," he said with a chuckle.

After her father left to smoke his afternoon cigar, Emily shared the details of the Sunday school lesson with her mother. Carol was horrified.

"Oh, no, honey. That's not what we believe at all. Listen, I know that you are busy with school and tutoring, but let me give you some things to read when you can," her mother added.

Carol had been Allan's secretary when they first met. Against her family's wishes, she married Allan. She had hoped he would convert. He always said he wouldn't rule it out, and he wanted to honestly believe, not just for Carol's sake. Despite their belief differences, they maintained a happy marriage. Allan encouraged Carol to finish college, and even encouraged her interest in evangelical theology and apologetics. Though he was quick to dismiss both, when hearing Carol explain evangelical arguments, he admitted they were stronger than he thought.

Upstairs in her library, Carol eagerly scanned the shelves. Her face hurt from smiling. She was elated to have a study partner, especially her daughter. "Start with these," said Carol as she handed Emily well-worn copies of *The Bible and Homosexual Practice: Texts and Hermeneutics* and *Hell on Trial: The Case for Eternal Punishment*.

Later that evening, Emily met two childhood friends, Calvin and Catlin Weber. They were brother and sister twins. Almost as attractive as Emily, Catlin went out of her way *not* to try. She would go days without showering and refused any attempts from her mother to soften her look. She declared herself to be asexual, not because she believed herself to be, but because most people disapproved of it. Unlike his sister, Calvin was an introvert and a computer and gaming enthusiast. His few attempts at dating during his high school and college years had ended badly. His social interaction was limited to time spent with Catlin and Emily.

The three friends settled into a corner booth at the Oneness coffee shop that evening. With some trepidation, Emily related the story of her conversion to Calvin and Catlin. They were shocked.

"Wait. That preacher guy that came here yesterday? Emily, are you sure about this?"

Emily assured the brother and sister she was indeed sure. After a few more minutes of pleading, Catlin relented and tried to be happy for Emily.

"Well, there's one side-benefit to your conversion. It will infuriate most of the people here," said Catlin.

Emily sighed but felt secure in her newfound faith. She then went on to share some details of her Sunday school lesson with Catlin and Calvin. They raised their eyebrows in surprise.

"This is your mother's church?" Calvin asked.

Across the room, Blaine Winthrop was in deep conversation with the coffee shop manager and a few regular customers. Blaine had struck up a friendship with the manager and staff his first day in town. He told them he wanted to build bridges with the campus alternative community, and that he was a new kind of evangelical, unfocused on traditional evangelical prohibitions. The manager and staff welcomed Blaine an as ally. As the manager finished the details of the previous day's events, he was quick to add, "But at least this preacher didn't win any converts with his exclusionary appeal."

"I'm afraid he may have," said Blaine.

Blaine went on to share what had he learned about Emily's conversion from Amy that morning. The manager and staff recognized Emily's name almost immediately. They were momentarily speechless.

"Well, if it's who I think you're talking about, she's here a lot. I can't believe she would fall for such evangelical drivel. Wait. That's her over there," said the manager.

The three friends were winding up their conversation when Blaine, the manager, and staff members approached their booth.

"Emily? I thought I recognized you. We met this morning," Blaine said with an extended hand.

After introducing Blaine to Calvin and Catlin, Emily looked at the group. The manager began.

"I just wanted to apologize for the uproar yesterday. We occasionally get those types here. And listen, I hope he didn't bully or pressure you," the manager said with a sharp look at Emily.

Emily had to suppress a laugh. "Oh, no. No pressure at all here. From what I witnessed, the poor guy was well surrounded and shouted down. But I'm glad he came. Things are so clear to me now," Emily added as she produced the offending tract from her purse.

As if on cue, Blaine, the manager, and his cohorts recoiled from the tract as if it were a snake. The manager's eyes were wide with horror.

"Mind if I take a look?" Blaine asked as he reached for the odious tract.

Blaine shook his head in disapproval and gave the manager and staff knowing looks.

"This is not what we stand for. Just to make that clear," Blaine added.

"So, what exactly *do* you stand for?" asked Catlin with a furious look. The manager grabbed the tract and practically threw it at Catlin.

"Look, Emily. If this Christian drivel is the new you, then I'm afraid you're not welcome here," said the manager with a glare.

Emily was on the verge of tears and could say nothing. She only nodded her head. Catlin and even Calvin were boiling over. Catlin glared at the manager, before adding with her trademark acidity, "Do you wanna hear a good lesbian joke? That's not funny!" Catlin yelled as she grabbed Emily's hand and brushed past Blaine.

"Get out! All of you! Now!" the manager practically screamed.

"Gladly," added Calvin. "Your coffee was never that good anyway," as he poured out a half-full mug on the floor on his way out after his sister and Emily.

"See, I told you they wouldn't like you now," Catlin said as she and Calvin hugged Emily who was visibly shaking. She hated confrontations.

Inside the coffee shop, the manager assured the remaining customers that all was well. Blaine nodded as the manager spoke. Afterward, Blaine met with the manager and staff.

"This type of bigotry can't be tolerated in our community. Let's put a video together. I have an idea in mind," Blaine said to the attentive manager and staff.

CHAPTER 10

L ate that evening at his home in Middleville, Brother Davis sat at the desk in his study when he received a phone call.

"Reverend Davis? This is Ethan Hillberry calling from the *Gotham Times*. I hope I'm not calling too late. Listen. I'm going to send you an email with a response I've prepared. I need you to watch the video attached to the email, and then confirm your response to it. And if you could send the response tonight, that would great. Your counseling of poor Bradley that we reported in our previous story struck a chord with our readers. We wouldn't want anything to jeopardize the rapport you've established with our readership."

Davis hung up the phone with dread. He thought he sensed both hints of complimentary sarcasm and veiled threats in Hillberry's voice. He knew well that Bradley was a fictional creation that he had consented to at the price of favorable press coverage. Would that sensitive lie be exposed if he didn't comply with this latest request? He didn't think so, but he had more to lose from disclosure than Hillberry.

With a heavy sigh, Davis opened the laptop on his desk. He opened the video. He sighed once more. The video started with a message "Scott Thornton, Baptist lay preacher from Middleville, Texas. His message is one of intolerance towards those of other faiths and the LGBT community."

The video went on to show the cover of the Gospel tract Scott had handed out at Oneness. The carefully edited video cut to an angry looking Scott sliding a tract across the counter to the manager at Oneness. The next frame, which included audio, showed Scott singing and playing "Amazing Grace" with a look of even deeper anger. The video concluded with an appeal for tolerance and an end to "bigotry under the guise of evangelical outreach."

Davis watched the video again. He remembered meeting Scott and Jill. They had not been members long. Getting members interested in evangelicalism was difficult. He was loath to do anything that would discourage any evangelistic outreach. He read the prepared response to which he was being asked to consent. "Our ministry upholds the love of Christ in all forms of outreach. The communities we serve should know we oppose attempts to pit the evangelical community against those of other faiths or the LGBT community. We disassociate our ministry from the recent actions of one of our members at Oneness Coffee Shop near Texas Heritage University."

After reading the prepared response and reflecting on the video, Davis sank into his chair. The phone rang. He noticed the number was Ethan Hillberry's. He let the call go. He felt trapped. He knew he should call Scott before agreeing to any demands. If he didn't agree, he risked exposure as a liar and opportunist. He wished he had someone to confide in, but there was no one. He paced the room and then replied to the email, granting his approval to the prepared response. Almost immediately, Hillberry responded with a thank you message.

The next morning Scott sat in his kitchen reading the paper as Jill prepared his breakfast. As Scott began eating his eggs, Jill noticed a van parked outside the house.

"Is someone supposed to come by?" she asked.

Scott moved toward the front window and frowned as he did. It was a TV van. What were they doing here, he wondered? He went outside to investigate. Almost as soon as he stepped out the front door, a microphone and camera were in his face.

"Mr. Thornton, do you have any comment on the incident that occurred at Oneness coffee shop near Texas Heritage University?" a reporter asked.

"Well, I was there, Saturday. I'm not sure what you want me to comment on," Scott responded.

"Oneness coffee shop is known for catering to the LGBT community at Texas Heritage. In your street preaching and passing out your pamphlets, did you explicitly target the LGBT community at Texas Heritage?" the reporter questioned.

Scott was caught off guard. The accusations were coming at him from all directions. He didn't consider what he was doing to be street preaching, not that he objected to anyone doing that.

"I wasn't trying to target any one group, and I didn't know anything about the coffee shop," Scott added.

At this point, Jill emerged from the house. "Honey, what's all this about?" she asked.

"Mrs. Thornton? Do you approve of your husband's street preaching?" the reporter asked.

Jill looked at Scott, who looked troubled. "I'm not sure what you're talking about," she said as she pulled Scott back inside the house.

Inside the house, Jill closed the curtains. "Now tell me what happened," she asked Scott.

Scott followed Jill into the kitchen. "Okay, honey. Tell me. What's this about street preaching?" Jill asked.

Scott explained that he hadn't thought of what he did at Texas Heritage as street preaching, but he could see how it could be taken that way. As Scott described the full encounter at Oneness, the phone rang.

"Jill? This is Brenda Crabtree from First Baptist. We've met. I'm Pastor Crabtree's wife. Listen, I won't keep you. It looks like Scott may have, um, gotten into a bit of a confrontation last Saturday. We feel bad. My husband was supposed to go with Scott. We didn't realize he went by himself. Anyway, if there is anything we can do, let us know."

Jill hung up the phone and sighed. "Please go on," she asked Scott.

Scott went on to relate the events of Saturday. Jill listened intently, staring wide-eyed as Scott reached the end of the story.

"You're just *now* telling me this?" she objected.

"I thought that would be the end of it," Scott replied.

"Well, apparently it isn't. Look, you'd better get to work," Jill responded.

Scott leaned in to hug his wife as he started for the back door to avoid the reporters. Jill drew back and threw her up her hands. Scott shook his head and slipped out the door.

Scott drove his truck hurriedly around the block a time or two to avoid a car that he thought was following him. He made his way to a house where his crew was finishing a roofing job. His crew was already at work. He waved, and they waved back but with an uncharacteristic awkwardness.

As Scott reached into the back of his truck to gather his tools, he noticed the owner of the house approaching him.

"Scott, I'm glad I caught you," the owner said.

"Is anything wrong?" Scott asked.

The owner did not answer but only raised his eyebrows.

"Listen. I need to leave soon. I know that I told you that you could put a sign in our yard to advertise your work. But, well, I think it would be better if you didn't," the owner said with an uncomfortable look.

"Sure. Whatever you like, sir. It's your property. We just appreciate the work," Scott replied.

Before leaving Scott, the owner went on to ask how soon Scott and his crew would finish the roofing job. "We should wrap everything up today," Scott replied.

As the owner walked away, Scott's mind raced. The owner had seemed so pleased with his work and seemed interested in inspecting every detail. Now he seemed interested in having Scott and his crew off his property as quickly as possible.

It was then that Vincent, a member of Scott's crew, came down off the roof.

"Hey, man. It looks like you had quite a day Saturday."

Scott was taken aback. "Well, yes, I guess I did," he responded.

"Some news guy stopped by here to ask us for comment on the video. We didn't say nothing," Vincent said.

"Video? Um, what do you mean?" Scott asked.

"You haven't seen it, man?" Vincent asked with surprise.

Scott shook his head in the negative. Vincent reached into his shirt pocket for his phone and located the video in question.

As the video played, Scott shook his head. "That's not what happened. That's just not what happened," Scott said.

"Hey. We didn't say nothing," Vincent replied, as Scott's anger appeared to simmer.

"I know. I appreciate that," Scott said and patted Vincent on the back.

At Scott and Jill's home, Jill watched the video on her laptop in the kitchen. She also read Brother Davis's prepared response. Which of the two infuriated her more, she couldn't say. She was on the verge of calling Scott, and then on the edge of calling the church, but she did neither. She peered out the front window, then left the house.

Late that night, Scott arrived home. His wife was not on the couch waiting for him, as she usually was. He went into the kitchen. Jill had left a note for him, letting him know there was food in the fridge and that she had gone to bed early. Scott ate, then drifted off to sleep on the couch.

Scott awoke that morning to a familiar sound—his cell phone. It was still early.

"Scott? This is Police Chief Pitts. Sorry to call so early, but I wanted to get you before you left for the day. Look, I'm sorry about that video. I just wanted you to know we had nothing do with it here. We're on your side. I'd like to send one of my deputies out later today to talk with you."

Scott thanked Chief Pitts and agreed to meet with his deputy. He first wondered why the deputy needed to stop by, but then he realized the deputy would take his side of the story. Jill might see that the video didn't represent what happened.

* * *

In her dorm room, Emily watched the video of Scott over and over. She seemed to seethe a bit more with each view. She knew the contents to be false and wondered who would go to such lengths at misinterpreting reality. The scolding nature of the comments associated with the video angered her all the more. Many commentators, in apparent seriousness, derided Scott as representing "the troubling radicalism within evangelicalism." Others scoffed at his "cultural tone deafness." After reading and lamenting the comments, Emily had enough. She had to do something.

Emily walked into the local police station. As she did, most of the male heads pivoted in her general direction.

"Yes ma'am. What can we do for you?" said the officer on duty at the desk.

Emily explained the reason for her appearance at the station. The desk officer frowned. As Emily slowly repeated herself, Chief Pitts stepped up to the desk counter.

"I'll take it from here, cousin," he said as he patted the desk officer on the back.

Emily introduced herself to the chief and thanked him for taking time to talk with her.

"I couldn't help but overhear. This is about what happened last Saturday?" the chief asked. Emily nodded.

"Yes, sir. I was hoping you could help me contact the man who was at the coffee shop last Saturday," Emily responded.

"I believe I can help," said the chief. "But why is it you want to get in touch with him?"

Emily reached into her purse and pulled out the tract Scott had given her. "He gave me this. And because of it, I'm now a Christian," she responded.

The chief was speechless. He searched Emily's face for signs she was joking. There were none.

"That is great. I don't know what to say. And that doesn't happen too often, I'll tell ya. This fella will be delighted to talk with you."

The chief then proceeded to vent to Emily unleashing a flurry of profanity about the injustice of the video and the half-story of it. How he had contacted the press and given statements challenging the footage. None of his comments were published through any news outlet that he knew of. He paused intermittently to offer apologies for swearing in front of a Christian woman. Emily had to suppress a smirk. Being called a Christian woman was alien to her ears.

"Listen, Miss. I've asked one of my deputies to visit the Thornton's in Middleville this evening. I want to make things right with them. He was mistreated here, and now he's getting a raw deal with this video. That bothers me," the chief continued.

The chief then tapped his desk as if to silence himself. He stuck his head out of his office. "Son, come in here," he called to Lieutenant Brad Cash.

"Miss, this is Lieutenant Cash. I've asked him to visit the Thornton's tonight," Chief Pitts added.

Brad shook Emily's hand as his eyes widened at her beauty. For her part, Emily introduced herself and noticed how tall and handsome the Lieutenant was. Chief Pitts smiled to himself, as he explained Emily's connection to Scott Thornton. Brad continued to smile at Emily and nodded in approval at the news. He arranged a time to meet Emily at her dorm that evening.

"You can thank me later. Maybe work some unpaid overtime?" the chief said with a laugh and a wink at Brad after Emily left.

Back in her dorm room, Emily combed her hair and checked her lipstick in the mirror. Catlin had stopped by to visit. "I don't remember seeing you wear that much lipstick. This guy must have made quite the impression," said Catlin.

Emily smiled as she continued to get ready.

"I can see it now. You're going to be a cop's wife with big hair and six kids," Catlin joked with Emily.

"Stop. You'll make my mascara run," Emily said with a laugh.

"Well, I *do* declare, honey," responded Catlin, as she imitated Emily's Southern belle manner.

"I have to size him up. He must meet with my approval," she said with a smirk.

As Brad pulled in front of Emily's dorm in his pickup, Catlin sat outside the dorm, smoking and appearing disinterested. In the passenger's seat of the truck, Emily glanced at Catlin. She flashed a rare, sarcasm-free smile and gave Emily a thumbs-up.

Jill had talked with Chief Pitts earlier that day. He apologized for the way Scott was treated, and he hoped to show her and Scott the genuine hospitality of the Texas Heritage Community.

"Ma'am, if it would be okay, I'd like to send one of my deputies by this evening to talk with you and Scott. And he'll have a young lady with him that I think you'll be interested in hearing from," Chief Pitts said.

Scott helped Jill with dinner. She felt more at ease after talking with Chief Pitts and began to allow Scott to hug her once more. As Jill set the table, the doorbell rang.

Brad introduced himself and then Emily. Jill couldn't recall seeing a more attractive woman than Emily. She glanced at her husband, who looked at Emily as if he recognized her.

Over dinner, Emily shared with Scott the story of how his tract helped lead to her conversion. Scott had to suppress tears at the news. Jill kissed him and smiled adoringly at Emily and Brad. She needed this news as much as her husband did.

Scott thanked Emily over and over. She went on to make clear to Jill that the video that went viral misrepresented what happened. Jill looked sympathetically at her husband.

"This whole thing with the video and the press must be real upsetting for you," Brad said looking at Scott and then Jill as they both nodded. "Speaking for my boss (and for me), we want to make things right for you. The chief is frustrated with the video and the press coverage. We wish there was something we could do," Brad added.

"Well, I wasn't going to say this, but it has been tough on both of us. In fact, one of my customers asked me to remove my business sign from his yard. He didn't say why, but I figured it out," Scott said.

"Honey, you didn't tell me this!" Jill replied.

Brad shook his head, but then assumed a resolute look.

"I tell you what. I don't know how set you all are in this area, but there's plenty of roofing work around Texas Heritage. You'll have all you can handle. The chief will see to that. He knows everyone in town. Listen. Think it over and call the chief. He wants to help," Brad noted.

After Brad and Emily left, Jill playfully eyed her husband. "Now I see why you wanted to take this campus witnessing trip," she said while tickling her husband who laughed and tickled back.

Brad couldn't stop staring at Emily all evening. She looked so good. To prolong their drive back, they decided to stop off for coffee at a Middleville diner.

Over coffee at the diner, Brad shared his life and love of his work, his church, hunting, fishing, and country music. Emily shared her love of literature, her family, and her newfound faith. She was struck that Brad seemed so non-threatened by her background. Many guys she dated would fall over themselves in attempts to impress her with their intellect. She still laughed with her father at the memory of a graduate student who kept referring to a Hobbesian choice (as opposed to a Hobson's choice).

As Emily enjoyed listening to Brad's love of Merle Haggard's music, she noticed an Asian woman approach the counter of the diner. The woman looked around quickly as she handed the waitress behind the counter an envelope. The waitress nodded and gave the woman a concerned look.

"What is it?" Scott asked as he noticed Emily glancing over his shoulder.

"It's nothing. Sorry," she said as she glanced at the woman quickly leaving the diner.

Not long after Brad and Emily left the diner, Eian arrived. The waitress behind the counter handed him the envelope the woman had left. He opened it slowly and glanced around him. His eyes stared wide-eyed at the message inside the envelope.

CHAPTER 11

As time went by, Emily and Brad saw more of each other and drew closer. He wasn't the type of guy her parents would select for her, but they both approved of him. Emily's father and Brad on more than one occasion would share a Sunday afternoon cigar and talk local politics.

Gradually, Emily began to slip into somewhat of a routine. She would spend Friday nights with Brad, and attend church with her mother on Sunday. Saturdays, she would tutor students or spend time with Catlin and Calvin, both of whom approved of Brad after spending time with him. Catlin would feel Brad's muscles and test to see if he could take a surprise gut-punch from her. With Brad's encouragement, Calvin began to volunteer his time at the police station as an ethical computer hacker.

One Saturday afternoon as Emily prepared to meet Catlin for coffee, her mother called. "Honey, listen. I need to run to the store to get some things for tomorrow's church potluck. Can you take Miss Maria home?" to which Emily agreed.

Maria was a Hispanic woman who helped Carol with house cleaning. She had been working for the family since Emily was in high school. As Emily drove Maria home, she was struck by the contrast between Maria's neighborhood and her own.

Emily pulled up to the curb in front of Maria's house. Over her objections, she began to help her unload some food items that Carol had given to Maria and her family. "Thank you, Emily," Maria said as Emily helped her.

As Maria unpacked the food items in the kitchen, Maria's teenage daughters, Mia and Daniela, came into the kitchen to see their visitor. Emily smiled at them. They smiled shyly back. "Say 'hi' to Miss Emily. Go on. Can you talk?" Maria said to her daughters who went meekly into the other room.

At Maria's request, Emily stayed for coffee. Maria gradually confided in Emily about her husband who worked construction and landscaping on Sundays and her son who was in prison. She worried about her daughters. She couldn't be there enough for them, and they needed guidance.

"Maybe I could help?" Emily suggested to Maria.

"Oh, no, Emily. You're so busy. You don't want to do that," Maria responded.

Emily insisted that she could find the time. Maria smiled and held back tears. Before leaving, Emily arranged to spend time with Mia and Daniela the following Saturday.

That Saturday, Emily took the girls out for lunch and then shopping. She was careful not to buy them anything that their parents couldn't reasonably afford. This became a weekly routine. After lunch, she would help them study and talk to them about hair, makeup, and boys.

In a brief time, noticeable improvement occurred in Mia's and Daniela's school work. They seemed more confident. Other mothers in Maria's neighborhood approached her about having Emily tutor their daughters. Emily agreed to take two other girls on while she looked for fellow students to help other girls. The mothers of these girls were delighted with Emily, and even more so as their daughters' confidence and performance improved at school.

While Maria was delighted with the progress her girls were making, she continued to worry about her son Hector in prison. She would on occasion share her concerns with Emily. After hearing about Hector and seeing how worried Maria was, she decided to visit him in prison. Brad did his best to dissuade her from the idea, as did her parents, but Emily assured them she would be fine.

The next Sunday afternoon, Brad drove Emily to the county jail to visit Hector. Brad had alerted the warden that Hector would have a visitor that afternoon. Emily had made cookies for Hector. She also had some drawings that Mia and Daniela had made for him.

Inside the prison, Hector had proven to be a hard case. To keep him from harming other inmates and guards, he at times had to be isolated. It even proved necessary to handcuff him to the bars of his jail cell. This, at least, gave the guards a fighting chance when forced to handle him.

Brad led Emily into the visitor's area of the prison. While family members could greet some inmates in an open room, Hector could only meet visitors behind glass. Two beefy guards led Hector up to a chair behind the glass. One hand and both feet were handcuffed to the chair, which was bolted to the floor. The guards positioned a microphone in front of him. Hector glared at Emily and still more at Brad.

On the other side of the glass, Emily greeted Hector. He replied back with profanity in Spanish. Emily scolded him in Spanish. She caught the slightest hint of a smile from him. Emily showed Hector the cookies that she had made for him. He nodded. She then showed him the drawings that Mia and Daniela had made. He betrayed a slight smile. Emily then prayed the Lord's Prayer in Spanish. Hector looked surprised. She then read Psalm 23 in Spanish. Lastly, she sang in Spanish a brief portion of "Amazing Grace."

"Your voice is nice, Sister," Hector responded in English for the first time.

Emily had forgotten that she was wearing all black, as she often did. Perhaps Hector had called her Sister without thinking. But he had not. But the name, Sister, stuck. Henceforth, Sister Emily was her name to Hector and throughout the prison.

As Emily left the prison with Brad, he could only shake his head. "What is it?" Emily asked with a smile.

"That is the toughest guy there. You got through to him," Brad said with an adoring look at her.

"I'm a tough Texan," she said, wrapping her arms around Brad's arm.

Emily began to visit Hector on a weekly basis. He soon asked for a copy of the New Testament in Spanish. In addition to the Lord's Prayer and a Psalm reading, Emily would try to answer questions Hector had about the Bible.

Soon other prisoners wanted to talk with Sister Emily. She took on as many as she could. As the weeks went by, however, it became apparent that she couldn't accommodate all the prisoners wanting to talk with her. She asked the prisoners with whom she met and the prison officials if she could meet with prisoners as a group. All agreed.

The prison officials, psychologist, and visiting chaplains all marveled at Emily's success with the prisoners. Invariably, each inmate that she met with soon began showing a marked improvement in behavior. Emily tried to explain her approach, but she admitted she had no formal training. Observers watching and listening to her on hidden camera were struck by the simplicity of her approach. They could only conclude that Emily's femininity and complete lack of pretense struck a chord with the inmates.

Emily would meet with a group of the prisoners in a common room. Sitting on a slightly raised platform, she would lead the men in scripture readings, songs, and the Lord's Prayer, before giving them a brief devotion. The guards would stand by for Emily's protection, but they felt they weren't needed. When Emily talked, the men listened with rapt attention.

One Saturday, as Emily began her talk with the men, Billy, a relatively new inmate joined the group. Billy whistled. Then he added, "The things I could do to you, preacher lady."

Nate, a heavily tattooed and muscular prisoner, stood and glared at Billy.

Emily stepped down and touched Nate's arm. "I'm okay, Nate," she said.

"I'm sorry, man. I didn't know she was your girl," Billy said looking nervously at Nate.

"You just keep talking," Nate said with a continued glare.

"Really, I'm all right," Emily added, touching Nate's arm once more.

The guards stood ready. They escorted Billy back to his cell. It soon became apparent to them that rather than protect Emily from the inmates, they had to protect those prisoners from harm who disrespected Sister Emily. It became so much of a concern that Emily had to address it herself, telling the men she was there to help them. And that they should only fight in self-defense, and never start a fight, especially over her.

Emily's work among the prisoners came to the attention of local media. A camera crew filmed her in the prison talking with the men. Her parents, friends, and Brad were all so proud of her. University officials were pleased with the social welfare aspects of Emily's outreach program, even though they disapproved of the evangelical faith underlying it.

The story in the local paper quickly made national news. Emily was happy with the attention as long as it somehow helped the prisoners. One Saturday morning as she waited for Brad to drive her to the prison, she read an article about her ministry on the *Gotham Times* website. Its title startled her. "New Directions: 'Sister Emily' and the Changing Face of Evangelicalism," the title read. The article's lead further troubled her. "While the past generation of evangelicals was content to hug the shores of pro-life activism and embrace the soft bigotry of 'love the sinner, hate the sin' relative to the LGBT community, Miss Emily Rosenthal has reached out in love to the incarcerated," the article began. Emily was puzzled. She had never thought of her ministry in relation to abortion or the LGBT community. The unspoken implication of the article was that she somehow took an anti-evangelical stance on these issues. As she pondered this, her phone rang.

"I'll be right down, sweetheart," Emily said thinking it was Brad and not checking the number.

"Miss Rosenthal? This is Herb Holt calling from Madison Cosmetics," the caller said.

"Oh, I'm sorry. I thought you were my boyfriend," Emily laughed and the caller laughed.

"It's quite all right. Listen. I won't keep you. I'm calling to let you know that we at Madison would like to sign you as a model for our winter brands," said Herb.

"Wait. I'm flattered, but I don't know that I can leave school," said Emily as she wondered if the call was a prank.

"We thought that. And we also know that you are quite busy outside of school. That's why we'd like to send a photographer to you. If you like the shots, we'll ask you to sign with us. Think it over, and I'll call back soon," Herb added.

Emily shared the news with Brad. He beamed. "Yeah, you should definitely do it, babe," he said with quick nods of his head.

It was settled. A Madison Cosmetics photographer arrived on campus the following week. He took several headshots of Emily in her black turtleneck wearing a brand of lipstick from the company. Emily was pleased with the shots. Herb Holt was more than pleased. Emily signed as a model with the company. It wasn't long before

Emily's likeness began appearing on billboards and downtown buses. She was overwhelmed. It was so unexpected and unplanned.

During her time in the prison, Emily lobbied for expanded vocational training for the prisoners. Prison officials did their best to accommodate this and any other request Emily made. Both officials and inmates had come to depend on her. Yet there was a limit to funding resources. With this in mind, using the funds from her modeling contract, Emily established a foundation for the prisoners and their families.

The foundation covered job training both for prisoners still serving time and for those transitioning to life on the outside. The needs of children of inmates were considered as well, with tutoring and mentoring services available for the children. Emily directed resources to at-risk youth in the community.

Scott and Jill Thornton had recently begun to help Emily with her prison foundation. They had recently relocated to the area. Scott trained and employed as many former inmates as he could in his expanding roofing business. In addition to employing released prisoners, Scott often joined Emily in the prison. His guitar playing became a favorite feature of Emily's group sessions with the prisoners.

The prisoners could not be any prouder of Emily. In fact, they began to revere her to a troubling degree. Emily heard reports of one prisoner who had built a makeshift shrine in his cell, using one of Emily's modeling pictures. He was observed kneeling before the picture. In response to this and similar reports, Emily did all she could to convince the inmates that she was no better than they. They would nod their heads in agreement, but their minds found it difficult to accept. They lived in a world where people were seen as good or evil, with little ambiguity in between. Soon though, Emily's focus would shift to a world in which the line between truth and falsehood was shadowy at best.

CHAPTER 12

During her senior year, Emily's light class schedule allowed her to spend a considerable amount of time with Brad, friends, family, and her new foundation. It and the notoriety from her modeling career turned her into something of a campus celebrity. What drew an ever-increasing group of male and female students to her was her evangelical faith. It seemed so out of step with her persona and the faithlessness of most of her fellow liberal arts majors.

Late one Thursday evening, Catlin stopped by Emily's dorm room. As she opened the door, she noticed two younger female undergraduates talking with Emily. The three appeared to be studying the Bible.

"Oh, I'm sorry. Is this a bad time?" Catlin asked.

"Not at all," Emily said, as she introduced Catlin to Amy and Cindy.

Catlin smiled before taking a seat on the rug. She then exhaled. All eyes were on a bag she sat down beside her. Sensing she had an audience, Catlin plunged into a recap of her evening.

"I've been doing some undercover work at tonight's Out meeting," Catlin said as she reached into her bag and pulled out a wig and sunglasses.

Catlin removed her customary pageboy hat and fitted herself in the wig and sunglasses.

"Wow, they look great. Seriously," Emily said in all genuineness, as Amy and Cindy nodded in agreement.

"Really? Thanks," added Catlin.

"How did you end up at an Out meeting?" Emily asked.

"It's complicated. Basically, Amanda gave me her "lesbian persecution complex," as if I know nothing of her suffering," she added, to laughter from her audience.

"The meeting was painful. That Oneness manager guy got up and said he wondered how people are heterosexual. No, I'm not kidding," she continued.

"Do you think anyone recognized you?" Emily asked.

"I don't think so. A couple of people smiled at my sunglasses. But there were a couple of frat guys there in disguise also," Catlin added.

"But the reason I came by is to tell you that Blaine Winthrop (that preacher guy) was there. And, get this: He introduced a gay couple that he plans to marry on campus at the Evangelical Student Union," Catlin added, to Emily's shock.

"Wow. I'm at a loss. I didn't think that he was a theological conservative, but I never suspected this. What did he say? And what was the reaction?" Emily asked.

"Everyone clapped, except me. I don't want their approval, even in disguise. But Blaine said he thought it was time to make a statement on campus. He thinks most of the students and faculty are on his side. And those that aren't 'need to move into the 21st century' and recognize marriage equality like the rest of the nation.'"

Emily shook her head as Amy and Cindy looked to her for guidance on how to react to the news. Emily looked up and noticed their looks and now a similar look from Catlin.

"What is it?" Emily asked, eying all three of them.

"Emily, people look up to you. You are a spiritual leader on campus now. Look, I know you're busy with Brad and the foundation, but you are needed around here more than you know." Catlin said in rare earnestness.

Emily's eyes watered. She had not thought of Catlin being remotely interested in Christianity, least of all evangelical Christianity. But she had been wrong.

"I appreciate that. I don't know what I can add or how I can help, but I'll try," Emily added, drying her eyes.

After Amy and Cindy hugged Emily goodbye, Emily queried Catlin further. As Emily gathered her thoughts, she noticed Catlin fiddling with her watch.

"Is that new?" Emily asked.

"Yeah, I needed this for my sleuthing. Everything that was said at the Out meeting was recorded," Catlin added tapping the watch.

Emily looked startled. Catlin went to Emily's desk. There she attached the watch to a USB port on Emily's computer. They both watched what was said at the Out meeting. It was just as Catlin had said. Blaine had a triumphant air about him, as he proclaimed himself part of a "new generation of evangelicals on the right side of history."

"Wow. You were right. Blaine is craving acceptance. I can't believe he believes all that. But he does." Emily nodded in resignation.

"Hey, be tough, Emily. Besides, you have to start preparing for your first God Talk meeting." Catlin added with a grin.

"My what?" Emily added with fixed curiosity.

"Check your email," Catlin added.

Emily opened her email. Catlin had sent her an attachment. It read, "God Talk with Sister Emily Rosenthal. Come and share in this weekly discussion. Time: Tuesday evenings at 7:00. Place: Campus Chapel. Warning: Attendance will challenge groupthink and may cause conversion to Christianity. Attend at your own risk! This week's topic: A discussion of Robert Gagnon's *The Bible and Homosexual Practice*. Be there for a discussion that will be offensive in all the right ways."

"Catlin, please tell me no one else knows about this," Emily stared.

"Sorry. I'm afraid everyone does by now," Catlin added feigning a worried look.

"What have you gotten me into, you?" Emily responded with a laugh.

"I didn't think you'd mind. And I thought it was a good time and place, and of course, a great topic, since I know that you've read the book. Look. I don't want to get emotional again, but you are needed. Guys like Blaine are turning the likes of Amy and Cindy into a bunch of zombies. They repeat the same mantras, like

#ProLifeNotJustProBirth as if on cue. If I didn't know better, I'd think the body snatchers had landed on campus," Catlin continued.

"All right. If you think this will be helpful. Your announcement should bring out the protesters in force, though," Emily added with a partial laugh.

"Brad has already taken care of that. Don't worry," Catlin added.

"Brad is in on this? What's he doing?" Emily asked.

"Don't worry. He's excited for you. And your ex-prisoner friends are too. They adore you. No one is going to get near you, uninvited. Trust me," Catlin explained to Emily, who looked concerned.

As Tuesday evening approached, the excitement and tension were building all week on campus. Blaine Winthrop established a Tuesday evening discussion at the Evangelical Student Union to counter Emily's meeting. In anticipation of protests, Catlin and Calvin infiltrated Blaine's group with informants. Blaine and his followers showed their cards.

On the appointed night near the appointed location, a small army of ex-prisoners stood in, with arms locked. No one could enter the narrow passage to the chapel unless they were granted admittance. Inside the chapel, a small group of ex-prisoners surrounded Emily, who was seated at the front of the chapel. Even with this tight security, the chapel was full.

Brad was seated in the front row with a loaded gun in his boot. As he sat smiling at Emily and looking around the filled chapel with pride, his thoughts raced. He had come to trust the prisoners with Emily. Oddly enough, he worried about her safety on campus. Catlin's announcement was provocative, but a rational, non-hysterical discussion about homosexuality and the Bible should be able to be held without fear. But that wasn't the case. There was no logic to the crowd psychology of the protesters.

Emily smiled at Brad, her bodyguards, and those in attendance as she began.

"Thank you all for coming. As you know, our presence here this evening and our topic for discussion have generated some interest on campus," Emily said, to sounds of barely suppressed laughter from the audience.

Emily began the discussion with prayer. There was dead silence as she prayed. She continued somewhat apologetically.

"Leading a discussion group like this is new for me. I'm not sure where or how to begin. This is a bit awkward, but I'll read my summary of the book. Yes, I will read it. It will save us time and hopefully be clearer.

"To summarize, Gagnon provides us with an exhaustive defense of Scripture's proscription against homosexual sex. He makes it clear throughout that the Bible doesn't oppose the impulse to have same-sex intercourse, but the act itself. His study of Old Testament texts offers an informative look at male temple prostitutes. For a fee, they would allow themselves to be penetrated by men. They would dress like women and even castrate themselves in some cases. The men penetrating them were thought to receive a pagan blessing.

"Gagnon's study of New Testament texts is equally informative. He undercuts various attempts to silence Scripture's warnings against homosexual sex, such as 'Paul was only concerned with exploitive forms of homosexuality, not stable relationships.' Using both biblical and pagan texts, Gagnon shows that although there were exploitive forms of homosexuality in the Ancient World, pederasty was thought to be a noble pursuit, and stable relationships between young boys and men were common. Gagnon also undercuts popular attempts to justify gay sex within the church, based on the church's willingness to tolerate divorce. He clearly shows that homosexual sex is *never* permitted in the Bible under any circumstances, but divorce is permitted in some circumstances.

"Also, Gagnon shows the health consequences for individuals and society, especially for homosexual men. Depression, AIDS, and suicidal thoughts are the risks associated with the gay population. Yet, gay activists want to make having multiple partners normative for the gay community.

"Written in 2001, Gagnon was prescient concerning the normalization of transgenderism. He also anticipated the labeling of those with a moral opposition to gay intercourse as bigots (akin to racists) and the threat to their careers. Gagnon himself has recently left his long-time professorship at Pittsburgh Theological Seminary, largely (it seems) due to the seminary's unhappiness with this Biblical belief against homosexual practice."

When Emily finished, Brad, Catlin, and Calvin all beamed, as did Amy and Cindy who were seated near the front. The rest of the audience sat in stunned silence. Some of them had grown up in evangelical churches. They had never heard anything like what Emily shared. Some of those who were not Christians had responses prepared. They now felt unable to respond.

"Now that we've all heard from me, I'd enjoy hearing from you," Emily said with a smile.

For a moment, there was silence. Then, a student near the front stood and began to speak. She asked Emily about same-sex attraction. Her own. Calmly, Emily told her that it was fine to have female friends, but that as a Christian, she could not act on her same-sex inclinations.

Another student asked about gay identity. Emily assured him that it was not necessary to see himself as gay, even if he had same-sex impulses. Even from a secular standpoint, she noted, there is a Kinsey scale of sexual attraction, ranging from 0 to 6. Only those at the 6 level are considered exclusively attracted to the same-sex, which is rare. Even if one finds himself or herself at that level, no one is under any compulsion to act on same-sex attraction, Emily explained.

"We're not responsible for our *attractions*. We're only responsible for how we *act* on them. Having a gay identity is unnecessary. Our identity and our humanity are found in Christ."

Still another student asked Emily why homosexuality should be regarded as any worse than any other sin. Emily noted that homosexuality violated the order of creation and the compatibility of male and female sex organs. Emily further pointed out that Christ considered Judas's sin to be greater than that of Pilate's. Hence, although we don't know the full impact of our sins, some have a more adverse impact than others.

As Emily concluded, she was swamped by people wanting to talk with her in private. With patience, she talked with each person. A couple of students wanted her to autograph one of her modeling pictures. Another wanted Emily to sign her Bible. She patiently agreed to the signings.

Talk of God Talk spread far and wide on campus all week. There was now not only a demand on campus, but a demand within the community to hear Emily. Given this, she decided to speak for two more evenings. The topics of her talks for those evenings came quickly to her.

In conversation with students on campus, a topic which came up, again and again, was hell. What did Emily believe about it? This was especially important because Blaine had been openly teaching annihilationism at the Evangelical Student Union. Students were confused. Was this acceptable to believe? Emily knew this aspect of the doctrine of hell needed to be addressed.

Another aspect of the doctrine of hell which continually presented itself in Emily's conversations with students was fear. People were flat out afraid of going to hell. It was that simple. It was not fear of the "unknown." It was a fear of a known—hell. Was belief in Christianity intended to alleviate this fear? Emily sensed the anxiety of the students and wanted to address it.

Even with two nights, the crowds to hear Emily were daunting. Every seat and aisle space was full. Students were seated on the platform. There were once again protesters outside the chapel, but their numbers were down from the week prior. Brad worried this meant that protesters were interspersed inside the chapel with the other students. He stationed campus police and ex-prisoners throughout the chapel and outside it.

To take the focus off her, Emily asked Scott Thornton to open in prayer and then play a short guitar instrumental. Emily quickly scanned the crowd before beginning to speak. She thought she noticed Blaine seated near the back, but she couldn't be sure.

"Thank you all for coming once again," Emily began. "It's a privilege for me to have the opportunity to talk with you all. Our topic for tonight is a difficult one. It's one many people struggle with, even those who have been Christians for many years. It's hell, not just the idea, but the overwhelming reality and finality of it.

"What do we mean by hell? Presbyterian Pastor Robert Peterson gives a clear idea based on the work of the medieval theologian Thomas Aquinas. He wrote that hell is both the 'pain of loss' and the 'pain of sense.' This, Aquinas based on Christ's words in Matthew 25:41. The condemned are ordered to depart from the presence of God into everlasting fire.1

"Why should we believe this terrifying reality? As one writer has noted, we must believe it based on the authority of Jesus. We can only accept hell on His authority. If we try to look past Him to our own emotions, doubts about the existence of hell or its duration will creep in until we believe something far less than what Christ taught.

"One notable departure from what Christ taught is what is known as annihilationism. This means the condemned will be punished for a time, after which they will cease to exist. Scripture teaches that there will be a resurrection of the condemned and the saved. Either way, our existence will continue after death. It will never end. Attempts to deny this are not new. As Augustine observed in his time, based on Matthew 25:46, Jesus taught that both the bliss of heaven and the misery of hell would be everlasting. As the bliss of heaven will never end, the pain of sense will never end in hell. We will always exist in one place or another. Likewise, the peace of gain will be unending in heaven, and the pain of loss will be unending in hell. To teach annihilationism is to provide false hope. Heaven is eternal peace, and hell is eternal hopelessness."

At this point in Emily's talk, Blaine stood from his hiding place near the back of the chapel.

"I believe in a God of love. It's a love we cannot escape from," he said with a raised hand.

"Thank you for joining us, Blaine," Emily responded. "Nothing I've said constricts the love of God. But if we love Him and believe He loves us, our first responsibility is to believe Him."

"I believe Him" Blaine retorted. "I believe Him enough to know we can't limit Him. He is free to act in any way that He wants."

"That's true, Blaine," Emily responded. "It doesn't apply in this case, though. Christ's teaching on hell was given to us to believe, not to look past with generalities offering misleading comfort."

Blaine then stood to leave. As he left, he asked everyone who believes in a God of love to follow him to the Evangelical Student Union.

"There we will pray for healing to come to our campus. There we will pray for an end to this spirit of division," he said, pointing to Emily.

Emily paused. "Anyone is free to leave with Blaine. It's up to you," she said.

As she finished the words, approximately twenty students followed Blaine out of the chapel. He paused to approach Emily, but he was stopped by Catlin. She gave him a deadly fake smile. He then turned and followed the other students out, shaking his head as he did.

"Now where were we?" Emily remarked.

"Anxiety and fear often accompany belief in hell," Emily continued. "Historian Kathryn Gin Lum has noted that in nineteenth-century America, ministers would warn of hell in hopes of having people rely on God's mercy for salvation. Sadly, though, 'some were unable to safely navigate the movement from anxiety to assurance' and suffered 'mental breakdowns and successful or attempted suicides.'2 God doesn't want anyone driven into mental illness or suicide over fears of hell. Its awful finality should drive us to believe and trust in Christ for salvation. Denying our fears or rationalizing away the finality of hell won't help us. Deep down, we know better. Yet just as fear of hell should be natural for us, God wants us to have assurance, not in ourselves but in Christ. If we look inward for assurance of our faith, doubts will ensue. Our confidence rests in turning toward Christ and his promise of salvation for us. We trust in Him and not in our faith, which may fail us."

As Emily concluded her talk, she paused to ask if there were any questions. A pensive hand was raised. Emily smiled and nodded at the student raising his hand.

He stood to ask, "Shouldn't we become Christians because we love God, not to escape hell?"

"That's an excellent point. Thank you," Emily responded. "We can only love God as Christians. So, it's not a love that any of us can have before becoming Christians. We do naturally fear death, though. Christ is the answer to this fear. We'll talk more about our love for God and others next week."

After her talk, Emily stayed late that night talking with dozens of students. So many wanted to talk with her that she had to address them in small groups. Yet she took her time with each person, being tenderly patient with each one.

CHAPTER 13

In the coming days, the reaction from Blaine and those students opposed to Emily's ministry on campus was fierce. Students aligned with Blaine harassed students seeming to agree with Emily's message. To these students facing harassment, Emily advised them to remain silent if the harassment was verbal, but to report any physical intimidation.

The opposition's narrative was subtle. They didn't outright challenge any part of Emily's message. To Blaine, she was well-intentioned but misdirected.

When asked by the campus newspaper about Emily's influence, Blaine indulged in vagaries.

"My faith is focused on this world, based on an inclusiveness centered on loving your neighbor as yourself," he shared. "Messages based on fear and emotion may yield short-term results, but students need a lasting faith. The loudest way isn't always the best way."

In considering her next topic for God Talk, Emily was mindful of the criticism Blaine and his ilk leveled against her, both in public and in private. She was conscious of many students looking to her for a response, and she felt the weight of this responsibility.

After some prayer and study, Emily decided the next God Talk theme would be "The True Meaning of Loving Your Neighbor as Yourself." As the crowd size for Emily's talks increased each week, so did the size of the protest. Brad and his group of former prisoners ensured that Emily was protected, but they had to enlist student and community volunteers to ensure the safety of crowds gathering to hear Emily.

As had become customary, Scott Thornton began the God Talk session with an acoustic guitar number. Emily then started her message. She scanned the crowd smiling at each face. They smiled back. There was hardly an empty space in the room.

"Thank you all so much for coming," Emily began. "What does it mean to truly love my neighbor as myself? That is our question for tonight. At first glance, the problem seems simple. We might take the answer to be that I meet the material needs of my neighbor in the same way that I would meet my own needs. Helping the disadvantaged in this way is one of the least controversial aspects of Christianity. Many non-Christians already agree that this is a good thing. As St. Augustine has observed, however, we must first address the question of how we love ourselves. Does loving myself mean that I meet my material needs? Certainly, we all should take basic care of ourselves, but surely Christ intended more than that. Well then, did Christ propose by his command that we buy ourselves nice things and are occupied with positive thoughts about ourselves? Surely not. Augustine explains how we are to truly love our neighbor as ourselves as follows:

'Now you love yourself suitably when you love God better than yourself. What, then, you aim at in yourself you must aim at in your neighbor, namely, that he may love God with a perfect affection. For you do not love him as yourself, unless you try to draw him to that good which you are yourself pursuing.' [1]

"As Augustine notes, I truly love my neighbor as myself when I love God and want my neighbor to have the same love for God that I do. Because each of us is naturally only interested in our own lives, how do we overcome this to love God and want this love for others? Lecturing on Augustine, Philip Cary has observed that our love of God is a gift from Him that we should ask for in prayer. We don't naturally love God, 'the love of God is shed abroad in our hearts by the Holy Ghost which is given unto us,' as is noted in Romans 5:5. This love for God and for others we can never know apart from Christ.

"From a secular standpoint, as Freud observed, I should love others as I love myself if they have qualities that I admire in myself. Or perhaps they lack these qualities but are part of my family, so I can love them. But what of strangers whom we don't admire, or who don't love us, and may not have our best interest at heart? According to Freud, such people are unworthy of our love and have more claim to our hatred.

"This is a bleak view. Yet it's one that the non-Christian world understands. As has been observed in the comic series, *Jessica Jones*, "no one can help anyone," [2] if helping someone is defined by his disinterested concern for others or our assessment of him as a 'good person.' In this dark space, the Golden Rule is something to avoid, because 'hell is other people,' as Sartre noted.

"Yet, in embracing the Golden Rule in its true sense, based on our love for God and wanting people to have the same love for Him, we recognize the worth of every person. It matters not whether a person is useful to us, has our best interest at heart, or is of noble character. We want every person to love God as we love Him."

The response to Emily's message overwhelmed her. So many students wanted to talk with her that, again, she was forced to address them in small groups. Brad looked on and could only marvel at what a natural Emily was in interacting with each student.

Word of Emily's God Talks spread across campus and into the surrounding community. There appeared to be so much interest that it became clear that the campus chapel could no longer hold the crowd, even with having her speak on two separate nights. Emily's father lobbied the administration for the use of the school basketball stadium. The administration agreed, reluctantly.

Catlin suggested to Emily that given the larger speaking venue, posters should be posted around campus announcing Emily's speaking engagement.

"And I suppose you have an idea in mind for this poster," Emily said, smiling at Catlin.

"Why yes, I *do,* Miss Emily," Catlin said while imitating Emily's Southern accent. Catlin then opened her book bag and pulled out her laptop. She showed Emily the poster that she had been working on. It was in the style of the Jesus People psychedelic poster art. Under a picture of Emily, the banner read as follows:

Sister Emily: The New Face of the Old-Time Religion

Texas Heritage Arena

December 2, 2018

Doors open at 7:00 p.m.

Emily loved the poster, as did Brad. Groups of student volunteers, former prisoners Emily had taught, and girls Emily had mentored all blanketed the campus and surrounding area with the posters. Blaine and his cohorts tried in vain to remove the signs. Each time they did, more appeared. Blaine was frustrated. A clear majority of the students had sided with Emily.

On the evening of December 2, a line formed outside the arena. Inside, security was tight with Brad placing fellow policeman throughout the arena. He wanted to surround Emily in bullet-proof glass. She thanked him but objected. Instead, a circle of former prisoners surrounded Emily on a raised platform in the middle of the basketball court.

The crowd filed into the arena. Despite the large venue, every seat in the arena was taken. Students, alumni, and members of the community all gathered. Sheriff Pitts looked at the crowd and could only shake his head. He had lived here all his life but had never seen anything like this.

As had become customary, the evening began with a guitar solo and prayer by Scott Thornton. The lights in the arena were dimmed. Emily went to the podium. One small light hung over her head. She was clad in her customary all-black outfit. The crowd of thousands was still. Emily began her message.

"The story is told of a young Frenchman approaching the French statesman, Talleyrand, during the French revolution. The young man had started a new religion in hopes that it would replace Christianity. Yet for all the young man's efforts, his religion failed to catch on. He asked Talleyrand what he could do to make his religion more popular in France. 'My dear fellow,' replied Talleyrand, my suggestion is to get yourself crucified and rise again the third day.' 3

Emily paused to take in what she could see of the crowd and then continued.

"Jesus' place in history is so secure that to even think of replacing Him is absurd. He lived and died. His burial tomb was found empty. His body was never found. Scripture tells us that Jesus rose from the dead. Over the centuries, many attempts have been made to deny the resurrection, introducing theories such as the body of Christ was stolen or Christ didn't die on the cross. Yet, these theories have been tried and found wanting. Christ did, indeed, rise from the dead.

"Jesus' resurrection in the body establishes His authority. Many great religious leaders have lived and died, and their teachings lived on after their death. Yet, Christ established the Christian religion by His resurrection. By it, we believe that Christ was God in the flesh.

"In our time, attempts are made to undermine the uniqueness of Christ under various banners of diversity, inclusiveness, and even social justice. By these, Christ merely becomes one option on the menu of choices in religion or philosophy. According to this thought, following Christianity may help society or bring social or health benefits to an individual. Christianity then becomes 'my most favorite way of living,' as one writer has observed. Such a shallow faith will never survive the stress of life or help anyone after death. Our predicament demands more.

"The predicament that we're in can be looked at in several ways. In Sartre's play, *No Exit*, three individuals die and go to hell. Sartre imagines hell as a hotel room. These three individuals are together joined in one room. One of the three knows precisely why she is there. At first, the two others are in denial, but then face the reality of why they are there. Sartre depicts the humanity of the three as an illusion.

"*No Exit* presents a bleak picture of where many of our contemporaries find themselves. A brutally honest handful of humanity knows it is headed for hell and deserves it. Many others cloak themselves in layers of denial, placing faith in family, friends, military service, or social work. Noble and good are all these areas of our lives, but we can't look to them for salvation, and our humanity can't be defined by them.

"Our humanity is defined in relation to God. Or as John Calvin once noted, 'no one can look upon himself without immediately turning his thoughts to the contemplation of God.'4 For all 'live and move' in God because we are created in His image. This is our humanity. Every life has meaning. This is the Christian basis for human rights, being pro-life, being for capital punishment, and being opposed to euthanasia.

"As Augustine observed, we were created in God's image, because we were created in the image of the Trinity—Father, Son, and Holy Spirit. As a result of the Fall, recorded in Genesis, our humanity has been tarnished by sin. Yet our humanity remains. Still, we inhabit a world clouded by the weight of sin, overwhelmed by disease, disasters, poverty, depression, murder, and suicide.

"In Milton's *Paradise Lost*, the Genesis Fall is told in poetic form. Adam and Eve sin, taking all of humanity with them. After their sin, Adam and Eve realize the full weight of their sin. Everything has changed for the worse. They are even estranged from the earth's animals, and its weather patterns turn against them. They contemplate bringing children into this bleak world. In the midst of Adam and Eve's despair, God shows His future salvation in Christ. Adam is allowed to see Paradise restored through the first and second comings of Christ.

"A world even more glorious than Eden awaits us in the New Earth after Christ's second coming. Yet to be part of this New Earth, the image of God in us that was tarnished in the Genesis Fall must be restored through faith in Christ. The robe of His righteousness covers our sin. We are then restored to a proper relationship with God the Father.

"Conversion to the Christian faith may take many forms. Each of us is different. For some, as in the case of St. Paul's conversion in the New Testament, conversion may be quite emotional and dramatic. For others, it may be neither of those things. The Baptist minister Charles Spurgeon once asked a young female parishioner what first drew her to Christ, and she replied as follows:

> 'It was Christ's lovely character that made me long to be His disciple. I saw how kind, how good, how disinterested, how self-sacrificing He was, and that made me feel how different I was. I thought "Oh, I am not like Jesus!" and that sent me to my room and I began to pray, and so I came to trust Him.'[5]

"If faith in Christ is so easy to realize, then we may wonder why anyone would object to it. There is only one good reason for objecting to the Christian faith. That is the problem of evil in the world. Or why does a good God allow evil to exist in the world? This is a question that has occupied the best minds in Christianity throughout its history. 'Since God is the highest good,' Augustine noted, 'He would not allow any evil to exist in His works, unless His omnipotence and goodness were such as to bring good even out of evil.'[6] In Genesis, God permitted Joseph to be sold into slavery by his brothers, so that God could work through Joseph's leadership in Egypt to save the lives of many by storing grain during bad harvest years.

"We may not always be able to see God bring good out of evil. Our perspective as humans is limited. But our perspective isn't God's perspective. Medieval Christian philosopher Boethius observed that God's perspective is eternal. Our view is finite. What time is it in eternity right now? There isn't time there, because it is always in the eternal present. God doesn't look forward or backward in time to acquire knowledge of events. He is outside of time, overlooking and knowing all of history at the same time. And he takes in all of history at once.

"From our vantage point of history, we observe that God permits evil, but will only allow it to continue so far. As President Lincoln stated in his second inaugural address during the Civil War:

'. . . American slavery is one of those offenses which, in the providence of God, must needs come, but which, having continued through His appointed time, He now wills to remove, and that He gives to both North and South this terrible war as the woe due to those by whom the offenses came...'

"The injustice of slavery was allowed to continue in America for so long, and then it ended. Hitler and Stalin held power and killed millions, but their power came to an end. So it is throughout history. God will only permit the duration of evil in history for so long.

"Beyond the problem of evil, there are many secondary reasons why people reject Christianity. But if they deny it, they reject it on Christianity's terms. It's mainly through the influence of Christianity in history that the concept of individual identity is recognized. In the ancient world before Christianity, religion was tied to the family and the state. Individuality was absorbed into the household gods, sacred fire, secret prayers, and other elements of a family faith, based on ancestor worship. Land could not be willed or sold but was passed on to male heirs, who were obligated to continue the family worship. Citizenship in a city was only realized within the family. The radical nature of Christianity with its allegiance to God, not the state, liberated humanity. True freedom was realized.

"The defiance of some in their rejection of Christianity may be intimidating. This cultural pressure has led to the marginalization of Christianity, even within evangelical circles. This pressure to go with the secular flow and blend in is an old one. Milton dramatized it in *Paradise Lost*.

"In Milton's story, he depicts the fall of Satan and his fallen angels from heaven. Satan tempts a group of angels to follow him. Shortly before Satan's fall, the angel Abdiel resists the will of Satan and his rebellion and chooses to remain loyal to God. Despite the pressure to rebel with others, Abdiel challenges Satan as follows:

Shalt thou give law to God, shalt thou dispute

With Him the points of liberty who made

Thee what thou art and formed the pow'rs of Heav'n

Such as He pleased and circumscribed their being?7

"While some may insult and attack Christianity, they are abusing the individual liberty God gave them. We must follow the courageous example of Abdiel and not yield to the desire for approval. God alone can give us this courage."

CHAPTER 14

L in sat in the executive lounge at Black Sands waiting for the day's meetings to finish in the ballroom. She was on edge but tried to mask it. She had thought of soothing her nerves with a drink but decided against it. She needed to keep a clear head.

As she had already notified Ethan in Middleville, she would not be joining the other company girls at the convention event in Houston. She was reaching company retirement age of 21 for her line of work. Beyond this, as she and the company both knew, she simply knew too much about the organization. Even in her retirement, she knew that Proteus didn't want to risk having her leave Black Sands. She had to find a good reason to ask permission to go, if only for a short time. She would figure it out from there.

Inside the ballroom, the day's presentations droned on. Seated near the back of the auditorium was Judson Kent II, a hard-drinking, big spending, wealthy Texan. Unlike most of the attendees, Kent had long since nodded off. He would occasionally wake up, notice that the presentations were still going on, then swear and go back to sleep.

Kent knew the drill with Proteus. Investors were shown the latest company breakthroughs in the morning presentations. But for the assumed promise of company-provided food, drink, and women, investors had to stay for all the presentations.

"Say, fella," Kent said to a nervous young man seated near him, "wake me up when he quits talking."

The day's meetings finally concluded, and Kent was roused from his slumber. He filed into the executive lounge with the other attendees. Although it was made to appear random, the company carefully orchestrated the evening. Each girl was assigned an investor in advance and given his background information. The girls had assigned seating areas where they were expected to make small talk over drinks and dinner with their clients.

Kent smiled as Lin introduced herself. "You don't mind if I leave my hat on, honey," Kent said as he snuggled next to Lin in the window booth.

Lin smiled. Inwardly, she was dreading what was expected of her later that night, but she had heard from the other girls that Kent was gentle. That eased her dread somewhat.

Kent was on his second Scotch and ice by the time the appetizer arrived.

"Sure you don't want some of this, honey?" he smiled as he dug into the cheese and bread.

"I didn't want to come out here. Daddy would have wanted me to, though. He stood by this place through some lean times. Lord knows why," Kent said, as he took another sip of whiskey and gazed at the desert landscape.

As Lin already knew, Kent's father had been one of Proteus's original investors. The company failed to produce a profit in its first years. It verged on bankruptcy during the dot-com bust years, and missed earnings several quarters thereafter. Still, Kent's father stood by the company. He told his friend Sam Jones that the company was the future, and not only would it turn the corner, but it would be one of the largest companies in the world. Kent's father proved correct.

"I can't quite see it from here," Kent said as he still looked out the window.

"What are you looking for?" Lin replied.

"Oh, it's a place my daddy built. I checked on it yesterday," Kent said.

"Wait. He built it out there? I didn't think there were any houses close by," Lin said.

"Well, this wouldn't show up on a map. It's underground. Daddy built it before this place was built. He was a little bit of a conspiracy theorist. He wanted a place for us to hole-up in when the government collapsed. He didn't think we could print money forever."

Lin was about to start drinking herself. With the news of this underground hideout, she instead reached for her water. She began to formulate a plan. But she needed Kent's help.

Lin wasn't sure if she could trust Kent, but she had to risk confiding in him.

"Listen, I need your help getting out of here. Really all the girls do. I can't explain everything now. Trust me and act like you're having the time of your life," Lin said with a fake smile.

Kent smiled and looked intently at Lin. He sighed and glanced around the room at the other girls. Each of them was entertaining a wealthy investor. The lesser side of Kent had been looking forward to spending some quality time with Lin. But like most Texans, Kent was a gentleman and a chivalrous one at that. He had suspected that something was amiss for the women working at Black Sands. Lin confirmed it. He had to help. It was a matter of honor.

"Don't you worry about a thing, honey," Kent said with a forced grin. "I'll get you out of here."

Lin smiled as she suppressed tears of excitement. She whispered to Kent that they should eat and appear as natural as possible. They were being watched. Kent suppressed a frown and began formulating his plan.

"Does everything meet with your satisfaction, Mr. Kent?" said a well-dressed Proteus employee assigned to supervise the evening's festivities.

"It most certainly does," Kent said flashing a wide grin at Lin who feigned embarrassment.

The Proteus employee nodded slowly in Lin's direction before moving on to the other tables. Lin forced herself to eat as the food arrived. Kent had lost his appetite but pretended to enjoy the meal.

Kent and Lin arrived in their penthouse suite. Both were tired and anxious. To Kent's horror, Lin had explained earlier that the suites were probably bugged or monitored on hidden camera. In the suite, they needed to fake being in the throes of passion.

Lin poured the two of them some champagne. Pretending to seduce Kent, she motioned him to the bed as she undressed. She turned off the lights and slipped into bed with him. As Lin had instructed, they both made a series of loud convincing groans, and then Kent pretended to snore. They both had to bury their heads in their pillows to suppress the giggles.

As Lin instructed, they both slept in and ordered a late break-fast the following morning. Kent had a plan. He would notify the organization that he planned to stay in town to gamble and that he had such a good time with Lin, he wanted her to accompany him to a nearby hotel casino. Although Lin had never been permitted to do such a thing, Kent was known to be a gambler. Most importantly, he was a longtime investor who needed to be placated. His request was granted.

Harris, Kent's limo driver, arrived at the room to transport their bags. He smiled at Lin as he entered the room. Kent tapped Harris's coat pocket to make sure he had his gun. He did. Harris gave Kent a questioning look. Kent winked at him and joked about the neighborhood being bad.

Inside the limo, Kent filled in Harris on the change of plans. Harris nodded in approval. He smiled at Lin. They drove to the nearby casino resort town, which the company had established to entertain investors.

About halfway through the journey, the limo paused long enough at the bottom of a hill for the three to exit the vehicle. The limo was equipped with a self-driving capability and Harris had pro-grammed it to proceed in the direction of the casino slowly. Harris took a few steps off the road, uncovered a keypad covered by brush, and a door opened on the side of the hill. The three slipped inside, and outside, the limo continued to advance on the desert road.

Once inside, Lin paused to look around. She was stunned. This place was like a luxury house. It was all buried into the side of a desert hill. Kent smiled at her. It pleased him that she was impressed.

"The limo should buy us some time, but we have to hurry," Harris said as he motioned to the far emergency exit.

The three exited the luxury survival bunker and were inside the emergency exit tunnel. There sat an old Cadillac. The three hurried inside. Harris quickly drove to the end of the tunnel. As they reached the surface, he hit a button. The exit door opened on the side of a fake boulder. The Cadillac headed quickly to the airport.

A company drone measured the limo's progress to the casino. The drone's findings were sent back to company headquarters. There security specialists wondered why the car was proceeding so slowly but decided to let it go.

At the airport, Harris quickly drove to Kent's jet. He got out of the car and hurriedly lowered the jet's ladder. Kent had not been scheduled to leave, so company security was not paying attention as Kent and Lin promptly went up the ladder and Harris drew it up behind them.

Kent settled into the pilot's chair and fired up the engines. Harris settled a nervous Lin into her seat, before strapping himself in for the quick exit. Kent quickly pointed the plane toward the runway. Inside, company security officials were alerted. They tried radio contact with the aircraft. No response. They immediately headed to the runway and drove in the direction of the plane with guns pointed. As they came within firing range of the aircraft, the Cadillac exploded in flames. The security team was nearly thrown to the ground. They could only watch helplessly as the aircraft lifted off the ground and took flight. As the plane gathered altitude, Kent's limo exploded on the desert road. Moments later the luxury survival bunker exploded, and the emergency exit tunnel collapsed under a heap of rubble.

Inside the plane, Lin sobbed. Harris held her hand. Kent turned and motioned her to the front of the aircraft.

"See. I told you I got this, honey," Kent said with a smile.

Lin kissed him on the cheek as she wiped away tears.

"Where to now?" Lin asked.

"Why to Middleville, Texas of course," Kent replied. "That's where your fella is."

CHAPTER 15

Kent was a longtime friend of Sam Jones's. He had a key to Jones's house in Middleville but had never used it until now. He was glad that he had the opportunity.

As daybreak came the following morning, Lin was still fast asleep in Eian's lap. Once in Middleville, she quickly found him. They talked, kissed, and hugged until they couldn't stay awake any longer. Jones's maid, Maria, had covered them up late that night and looked in on them early that morning.

Kent was sleeping soundly in one of the guest rooms. His driver was wide awake on the massive outdoor deck. He smoked and watched the sunrise. Maria bought him some coffee and offered him breakfast. As Maria went back inside to start breakfast, Kent woke up in his room. He was glad Lin was safe with Eian, but his mind raced. What about the girls still trapped inside Black Sands? This wasn't over for him, and he knew it wouldn't be for Sam Jones, once he learned the awful secrets at Black Sands.

* * *

Inside Black Sands, Proteus's CEO, William Whentworth, tried to remain calm. He should have seen this coming. He trusted Lin, and he thought Kent to be a bumbling man, absorbed by lewd self-interest. He had clearly misjudged both Lin and Kent. He pondered these thoughts as he sat smoking in his office plotting his next move.

At a large table in the basement of Black Sands sat Proteus's security team and the women within the organization assigned to entertain investors and new employees. Whentworth paced back and forth in front of the table smoking and glaring at the seated group. At the back of the room stood armed guards. A small window overlooked the center of the room.

"Well, now," Whentworth began. "Let's start from the beginning. After all that this organization has done for Miss Lin, she has chosen to betray us. I take this hard. She was special to me. One of you saw something. One of you knows something. Now is the time to share it. Who wants to begin?"

The seated group sat in fearful silence. After a full minute had passed, Whentworth pounded the table and lit another cigarette.

"Okay then, perhaps we need a little motivation," Whentworth added with a nod and a smile to one of the guards.

The guard stepped forward and approached the end of the table where one of the male security team members sat trying to keep a brave face. The guard glanced at Whentworth. He nodded. With this, the guard punched the security team member straight to the face. Blood dripped on to his uniform. At this, one of the girls gasped. Whentworth looked at her with raised eyebrows and a smirk.

"It appears as though Miss Ning has something that she would like to share," Whentworth said with a smile.

Ning related how Lin had confided in her about her unhappiness at Black Sands. She feared for her future. She feared for all the girls in the organization. And she desired to leave and help others go as soon as she could.

Whentworth smiled and nodded.

"Thank you, Miss Ning for coming forward," he said. "Never be afraid to confide in your supervisor or me if you should learn of any information like this in the future. This is a small reminder," Whentworth said as he stubbed his cigarette on the back of Ning's outstretched hand. She shrieked in pain as the other girls looked on, horrified.

Meanwhile, in the room overlooking the interrogation room, Ning's friend Chen, a chef at Black Sands, unplugged a thumb drive from one of the computers. She had managed to copy the video file of the entire interrogation. She heard footsteps outside the door. She hid in the closet and tried to quiet her breathing. Once the room was clear, she quickly left and took the stairs up to the kitchen. Inside her office in the kitchen, she transferred the video file to a laptop, and then to her phone. She then sent the video to Lin.

* * *

Lin was still in Eian's lap, but now awake. She heard her phone ping, indicating a new text message received. She kissed a still sleeping Eian and then reached for the phone. She recognized Chen's number and hoped nothing had happened to her. Chen's text was a short message to watch the attached video.

Lin watched the video in horror. She began to cry. Slowly, Eian was roused from his slumbers by her cries.

"What is it?" he asked.

Lin handed him the phone and told him to watch the video. Still crying, she buried her face in his chest. Eian watched the video in shock. It stunned him to see Whentworth in the position of a torturer. He felt equal sympathy for Lin and anger toward Whentworth. Eian wondered if Whentworth had somehow orchestrated the release of the video just to torment Lin.

Maria stepped in to check on Eian and Lin.

"Breakfast and coffee are downstairs," Maria said with a smile.

Over breakfast and coffee, Eian and Lin showed the video to Kent. His jaw tightened. He exhaled deeply before muttering curses under his breath.

"Hey, doll," Kent said to Maria. "What time is Sam due back?"

"Mr. Jones should be home in about an hour," Maria said checking her watch.

"Now I don't want you to worry about a thing, honey," Kent said to Lin. "When Mr. Sam comes in, we'll tackle this thing together. We'll take care of it, if it's the last thing I do."

Within the hour, Sam Jones pulled into the long drive in his convertible. His wife was occupied with charity concerns that day in Houston, and he was looking forward to golfing and talking with Mr. Simmons. Jones noticed a limo in the drive as he came in the front door where Maria met him.

"Who is driving that limo, Miss Maria?" Jones asked, looking into the kitchen.

"I thought that was you, Mr. Sam," Kent said.

"Well, look what the wind blew in," Jones said giving Kent a bear hug. "Glad you're here."

Jones stepped into the kitchen while Maria poured him coffee and warmed up a biscuit for him. Eian had stepped out of the kitchen momentarily, and Lin sat and rose to greet Jones.

"Now who is this lovely lady?" Jones said smiling broadly at Lin. "Don't tell me you got married again and didn't invite us."

Kent introduced Lin, then as Eian walked in, he introduced him also. Jones smiled cordially at both Eian and Lin. Maria brought him his coffee. He sat down wondering about the nature of the visit.

After another round of banter, Kent went on to explain why he, Eian, and Lin were there. Jones's eyes widened as Kent explained. Finally, Kent showed Jones the video that Lin had received from inside Black Sands. Jones stood up and paced the room, cursing lowly as he did.

"This shouldn't surprise me," Jones said. "But it does. But don't you two worry, we'll take care of it and you," Jones said addressing Eian and Lin.

Jones pulled Kent aside. "Listen. You remember meeting Mr. Simmons?" to which Kent nodded. "I'd like to pull him in on this."

* * *

On the other side of town, Brother Davis was in deep conversation with Mr. Simmons. Davis had called early that morning and needed to talk. It was urgent. Seated in Davis's study, Mr. Simmons listened to Davis. Mr. Simmons heard the until now concealed tale of the attempted rape of Becky Worthington and Jones's efforts with

Chief Weston to keep the scandal private. He also listened to the painful details of Davis's counseling with the fictional Bradley. Mr. Simmons was deeply disappointed but not surprised. He had sensed Davis was deeply troubled by something. Still, the full extent of the situation overwhelmed even him.

"Listen, preacher," Mr. Simmons said in earnest. "We need to make sure that this situation is handled well. I'd like to bring Sam Jones in on this," to which Brother Davis nodded in agreement.

Becky was starting her last class before lunch when the school secretary called her out of class. In the hallway, Alex and Samantha waited. The two led Becky outside where her father Darren waited.

"What is it, Dad?" Becky asked the three.

"It looks like you're finally going to get justice, girl," Samantha responded.

On the way to Sam Jones's house, the three filled Becky in on the details of what had happened. Mr. Simmons had called Becky's father, detailing his conversation with Brother Davis. He had also called the church secretary. Without going into detail, he asked her to discretely call Becky, Alex, and Samantha out of class. Relaying Mr. Simmons's instructions, they were told to go to Sam Jones's house. They would understand once they arrived there.

Inside Sam Jones's house, Jones sat with Becky, her father Darren, Alex, Samantha, Brother Davis, Mr. Simmons, and Chief Weston. Eian, Lin, and Kent talked in the kitchen with the door open.

"Something has come to my attention," Jones began. "Three young men in our community attempted to rape (let's call it what it is) this young lady," he said pointing to Becky.

Becky looked startled. Chief Weston looked embarrassed. Brother Davis looked ashamed. Alex, Samantha, and Becky's father all seemed relieved.

"Now I've been around a while," Jones continued. "I understand why things like this are swept under the rug. Doing that only hurts our community. More importantly, it denies justice to this young lady and her fine father. This has to be dealt with, and we all know what has to happen."

Brother Davis tried to deflect the blame away from Chief Weston. He said he selfishly feared the negative fallout on the church's nationally known ministry. He also added that he had already submitted his resignation to Mr. Simmons. Pastor Crabtree would now serve as pastor at First Baptist.

Eian couldn't help but overhear the conversation from the open kitchen door. As Brother Davis unburdened himself, he felt a nagging sense of his culpability in Davis's troubles. He whispered to Lin who nodded, following him into the living room with Kent in tow.

Chief Weston was about to speak when the three walked in from the kitchen. Everyone looked up.

"I couldn't help but overhear Brother Davis," Eian said. "I think I'm partly to blame for what happened."

Everyone looked startled. They recalled seeing Eian at church. How could he be involved in this? Eian answered the question. He explained how he had gone into Brother Davis's office and misrepresented himself as a Christian, as part of his job at Proteus.

"Proteus has a project targeting the evangelical community," Eian began. "I was placed here, directed to join the church, gather information, and ensure that the #ProLifeNotJustProBirth movement took root on the ground here, as it has elsewhere in evangelical churches across the country. This idea is the brainchild of Proteus. They attempt to influence the evangelical community by using algorithms. The goal is to influence evangelicals in a secular direction, away from evangelical beliefs. I wanted to come forward before now, but I was worried about what would happen to her," he said putting his arm around Lin.

Some of the group looked at Eian in disbelief. With no apparent profit motive, Proteus planted an employee in a church in Middleville, Texas. It seemed like the stuff of the wildest conspiracy theories. But as sensational as Eian's claims sounded, they made sense to Alex, Brother Davis, and Sam Jones.

Alex recalled the code that he had seen on the Proteus search page, which inexplicably had Brother Davis's name hard-coded into it. Brother Davis and Sam Jones suspected there were machinations behind First Baptist's improbable rise to national media attention, especially via the internet. Jones couldn't understand this from a profit perspective, though.

Alex went on to relate the bit of code that he had noticed on the Proteus search page and how it seemed to verify Eian's claims. Brother Davis and Sam Jones nodded. Lin looked proudly at Eian. The others looked on, absorbing the news.

"Although I was not a Christian before coming to Middleville, I am one now," Eian continued.

"In part, this is due to hearing and believing the messages of Brother Davis's sermons. I know justice must be done, but it's important (now more than ever) that Brother Davis remain as pastor at First Baptist. I'm afraid that Pastor Crabtree has bought into Proteus's objectives to undermine evangelicals. He is touting their agenda without realizing it."

No one said anything for a moment, until Sam Jones broke the silence.

"This young lady and her father still deserve justice," he began. "But in light of this new information, if it's left up to me, Brother Davis needs to stay on as pastor," he said looking at Mr. Simmons.

"It's up to Becky and her father," Mr. Simmons said, looking at both of them.

"I do want justice for Becky. What happened to her shouldn't happen to anyone. I'm fine with Brother Davis staying on as pastor if she is," Becky's father said.

Becky nodded in the affirmative to these words. She hugged her father, then hugged Alex and Samantha. Lastly, she hugged Brother Davis and Mr. Simmons. Brother Davis had tears in his eyes.

Later that evening, Jeff Taylor, Tad Smith, and Matt Nelson were each arrested at their parents' homes and taken into custody. For Becky's sake, every effort was made to hide her identity from the public. The three boys accepted a plea deal of no prison time in exchange for guilty pleas on charges of attempted rape.

With justice served for Becky, Jones and Kent moved to seek justice for Lin. Eian and Alex had a plan. Jones and Kent listened to it and agreed to act on it.

CHAPTER 16

Proteus CEO William Whentworth sat chatting with attendees at Tech Expo in Houston. Tech Expo was one of the few occasions on which he left Black Sands to appear in person. He loved the accolades. Subordinates cautioned him that in light of recent events, it might be better not to attend the Tech Expo this year. He ignored their advice, as he often did.

Whentworth had already given well-received remarks at the keynote session that morning. He was now set to deliver remarks in a break-out session called, "Women in Technology: Proteus Leads by Example." The room was packed. Leading industry executives, especially women, were in attendance. Whentworth reluctantly left the company of a young female executive to take the stage and begin his remarks. Before doing so, he was introduced by the panel chair, Dr. Amber Davies, a research specialist at Proteus and author of *Women Who Code: Overcoming Gender Bias in Hiring Practices.*

"It's my distinct honor and privilege," Dr. Davies began, "to introduce a dear friend and a leader in our community. He shares my hope and yours that the line outside the women's restroom for this conference will one day be as long as the line outside the men's room. Seriously though, this man believes in equality and in recognizing and rewarding female talent in the industry. I'm proud to work at Proteus and even prouder to introduce to you William Whentworth, CEO of Proteus."

The audience erupted in thunderous applause as Whentworth took the stage. He smiled and nodded to the crowd. He then began his presentation.

At the back of the room, Huan Wong, a conference employee, sat ready to load Whentworth's presentation. An opening slide already appeared on the screen. As Huan loaded a CD containing the main presentation slides, he received a text message. "Urgent! Report to the side entrance of the main stage. Problem with Whentworth's mic." Huan hesitated for a moment, loaded the CD, then left to go to the front of the room.

Huan reached the side entrance to the stage. There Samantha greeted him.

"Hi, you must be Huan," Samantha said with a bright smile and extended hand. "It looks like we have our technical problems under control. Thank you for coming on such short notice. Now that the presentation has started, maybe you can buy me some coffee. I'm a student, and I'm trying to take all this in," Samantha said, grabbing Huan's arm and leaning into him while flashing a bright smile.

Huan knew that he should go back to the control room to monitor the presentation, should anything go awry. It usually didn't, however, and Whentworth's presentation would likely go on for some time. He could slip out for a moment and make it look as though he had never left.

As Samantha led Huan from the conference room to the refreshment area, Alex slipped into the control room in the back of the room. Alex quickly switched the presentation from the CD with one loaded on a USB flash drive. There was a slight blip on the display screen seen by the audience, but few seemed to notice. Alex immediately left the control room and locked the door behind him.

After thanking Dr. Davies, the conference attendees, and the charming city of Houston, Whentworth began the slide portion of his presentation. Using the remote control slide advancer, he flipped to his second slide. As expected, the slide contained a searing indictment about the underrepresentation of women in the industry. "Patriarchy, Patrimony, and Privilege have excluded women from the IT industry," the slide began.

"We might use the term qualified women," Whentworth continued. "But for years it has been my practice to edit out the adjective, qualified, before the noun, women. The inclusion of this word represents a hidden form of sexism masquerading as equality. It carries with it the backward implication that women need a bit of help in excelling in our industry. That, my friends, as you well know, is far from the truth. We are past such backwardness. Women simply need to be given the opportunity to excel."

The crowd nodded in approval. Dr. Davies was on the verge of tears. "Isn't he wonderful," she said to her colleague.

"At Proteus, we have long understood the importance of fostering a culture of inclusion," Whentworth continued. "Which is why as you'll see here, over a third of our research employees are women. And as you'll note, that number is increasing with the number of female interns coming into the organization."

Whentworth paused to look at the crowd. Instead of the glowing approval that he had expected, awkward looks of confusion shown on faces in the crowd. He flashed a confident smile before turning to the slide presentation which read, "In the United States, one out of six women has experienced attempted or completed rape."1

Whentworth kept his composure. "Yes, we at Proteus, like all of you, have a zero-tolerance for violence against women. I had forgotten that aspect of my remarks." he continued.

He flipped to the next slide trying to appear as composed as possible. The next slide read, "Violence against women is the leading cause of injury of women between the ages of fifteen and forty-nine. Violence against women and girls crosses all borders, cultures and classes."2

Whentworth tried to appear calm, but he was now shaken. Audience members exchanged confused glances. He thought of abruptly ending his remarks, but he noticed that Dr. Davies continued to smile and nod in approval. He advanced to the next slide. He was trapped. To his horror and that of that audience, a video launched on the screen. There in full color, the conference attendees witnessed Whentworth extinguishing a cigarette on the back of Ning's outstretched hand. The video played over and over. The audience gasped. Whentworth lost all composure. He left the stage screaming obscenities. As he left, the screen went black. Through the speakers, the audience heard a deafening scream of "No!" It was Becky's scream during the attempted rape.

Outside the conference room, Huan heard the commotion inside. Was it over already? He wondered. He didn't see anyone coming out of the conference room. "I'd better get back inside," Huan said to a still smiling Samantha.

As Huan went inside the conference room, Whentworth was at the back of the room kicking and cursing the locked door of the audio-visual control room. The audio scream continued on repeat, seemingly growing louder. The audience was in complete disarray. Dr. Davies felt faint, but she went to the back of the room. Perhaps this was all some cruel joke, she wondered.

Huan fumbled for the keys to the control room, and Whentworth hurled curses at him. Dr. Davies approached Whentworth to calm him. He glared at her. She persisted. He nearly threw her to the ground. Huan began to unlock the door but paused to check on Dr. Davies. Whentworth took a swing at Huan, but Samantha blocked the punch. She then kicked Whentworth full force in his privates, sending him doubling over in pain. "Come on, let's go," Samantha said to Huan as she led him out of the room and outside into a waiting limo.

"Wait. What just happened and where are we going?" said a bemused Huan inside the limo.

"I'll explain everything. You'll see." Samantha said.

"Thanks for coming to my defense back there," Huan said with a grin.

"No problem," Samantha said flexing her bicep to a still grinning Huan.

Inside the conference room, Whentworth had forced his way into the control room and began trashing all the equipment. People were flooding out of the conference room in shock. Security arrived and pulled Whentworth out of the control room. Dr. Davies sat crying near the back of the room as colleagues tried to console her.

Later that day, Whentworth sat with a team of lawyers, his security team, and his junior staff, at a long table in his hotel suite. On the other side of the table sat Dr. Davies and an assortment of her influential friends, all of whom heard Whentworth's talk, saw the video, and witnessed his meltdown earlier that day. Whentworth's legal team proposed an agreement to Dr. Davies and her friends. In exchange for their silence, Proteus would pay each of them ten million dollars and an equal amount going to the charity of their choice. Dr. Davies agreed to the terms in silence. She and others signed their names to the agreement.

Whentworth arrived back at Black Sands late that evening. While sitting in his office, his mind raced over the day's events. He lit a cigarette and poured himself a drink. His cell phone pinged. He had a new text message, which read "Enjoyed your presentation today – Judson Kent II."

Whentworth seethed. He paced the room. "What do you want, Kent?" he replied back.

"Easy. Even for you. Let all the girls go and anyone else who wants to leave," Kent answered.

Whentworth paused for a moment. He hated to let anyone get the better of him, especially Kent. He had little choice, though. "Fine. Be here tomorrow at 0900," Whentworth responded.

Early the next morning at Black Sands, a fleet of black SUVs lined the entrance to the building. Kent stood outside with the drivers, all of whom were heavily armed. Quickly, all fourteen of the girls in the same line of work as Lin made their way to the front entrance. Chef Chen accompanied them. The women anxiously made their way into the SUVs. From his top floor window, Whentworth watched them pull away from the building and head out on the desert road.

In the coming days, Dr. Davies remained in her hotel room in Houston. She had trouble getting out of bed, let alone leaving the room. She knew that she couldn't stay there forever, but she was still in shock. Her mind couldn't focus. She kept repeating the events in the conference room. She kept seeing the awful video in her mind's eye, and with it, the rage on Whentworth's face as he nearly threw her to the conference room floor. She hated herself for agreeing to the settlement. But what troubled her most of all was the way the story played out in the media. The tale planted by Proteus seemed too far-cical to be believed. Yet believe it the media did. Dr. Davies turned on the television to hear the story once more.

"Tonight we learn more details about the activities of Project Truth at the Tech Expo event in Houston last week," the announcer read. "Sources tell Live News that Project Truth, known to target Unplanned Parenthood, may have targeted Proteus at Tech Expo. Project Truth reportedly hacked a presentation given by Proteus CEO William Whentworth. Huan Wong, believed to be working with Project Truth, fled the scene. It's not immediately clear why Project Truth would target Proteus. The organization is known as a leader in women's health issues. Joining us now from Boston is the Director of Unplanned Parenthood . . ."

Dr. Davies turned off the television in disgust and threw the remote across the room. She sank into her bed once more. She thought of taking another sleeping pill, perhaps more than one. As she reached for the pill bottle, there was a knock at the door. She peered through the peephole and saw two men, one of whom she vaguely recognized. She opened the door to find Sam Jones and Judson Kent standing in the doorway.

"Dr. Davies? I'm Sam Jones, and this is Judson Kent," Jones said. "I'm so glad we located you. Listen. We know everything that happened. We'd like to help you, and we need your help."

Sam Jones's house in Middleville was turned into a virtual girls' dormitory. Lin, Chen, and the other girls occupied the house, with Chen serving as a chef and Maria continuing to serve as a maid. Dr. Davies settled into the guest house but received frequent visits from Lin and the other girls. Huan and Eian moved in with Alex. Becky and Samantha made frequent visits to Alex's house, and the group made frequent trips to Jones's house to spend time with Lin and the other girls.

Jones and Kent wanted everyone to enjoy themselves. They both wanted to give Alex, Becky, and Samantha time to finish school. Also, Lin and the girls, as well as Dr. Davies, all needed time to heal and unwind. Jones and Kent let the group know that they were forming plans for a new company. Everyone was excited about starting a new chapter in their lives.

EPILOGUE

Months later, Whentworth sat in his office in Black Sands. He addressed his most trusted executives on plans for the company going forward.

"Gentlemen, we had some defections from the company last year, as you well know. We must face these setbacks, however momentary their nature. Yet in one all-important way, we proved ourselves last year. We proved that the beliefs of the evangelical public are malleable. We can form their beliefs and those of the public at large. Our task is to lobby for internet access across the country and the world. Our reach knows no limits. It is global. It could happen here in our lifetimes."

* * *

After graduation, with a grant from Sam Jones, Becky established a candy store in downtown Middleville. She began making plans for marriage to Alex, who proposed to her shortly after graduation. At the urging of Jones and Kent, Alex started working as a programmer in their new organization.

After graduation, Samantha opened the priciest restaurant in Middleville with a grant from Sam Jones, for whom she also served as a special assistant. She and Huan began dating and formed an unlikely love. Jones and Kent hired Huan as well.

Eian and Lin were married that summer at First Baptist with Brother Davis presiding. There was a lavish reception at Sam Jones's house for the pair. He sent them off on a London honeymoon, while Kent oversaw work on a new home for the couple. Eian would start work in Jones's and Kent's organization after his honeymoon.

Everyone decided that Lin and the other girls needed more time to heal. In fact, Jones and Kent wished that Lin and the other girls could work at home as wives and mothers. They had suffered enough at Proteus for one life. At Lin's encouragement, the other girls became Christians like her. And they were baptized and joined First Baptist with her.

Dr. Davies continued to live in the guest house on Jones's property. Jones and Kent hired her as a technical consultant. Dr. Davies formed a friendship with Chen from whom she began taking cooking classes. Chen also encouraged Dr. Davies to attend First Baptist with her. She did. There she met Emily's father, Darren, and the two began dating.

Brother Davis's ministry thrived like it never had. Unburdened by guilt, he felt years younger and approached his ministry with renewed vigor. Davis heard of Emily's evangelistic ministry at Texas Heritage. He invited her to First Baptist in Middleville to hold three nights of evangelistic services.

Emily and her now husband, Brad, were received with overwhelming favor at First Baptist. At the invitation of Mr. Simmons, Jones and Kent attended one of Emily's evangelistic services. Both men could not have been more impressed. With their financial backing, Emily and Brad traveled to college towns, big cities, and hamlets across the country. They flew Emily and Brad to all of Emily's speaking engagements and flew the pair back to Texas Heritage each Saturday.

One Saturday when Emily returned with Brad from a series of evangelistic meetings near the University of Illinois, Jones and Kent met the two at their home near the Texas Heritage campus.

"Miss Emily, we want you to keep doing what you're doing. It's vitally important," Jones began. "But we would like to hire you as a consultant, as you have time. We have the technical help we need. What we lack is someone with an evangelical edge to add content to our mission."

"Wow. I'm overwhelmed," Emily said with a smile. "What is your mission?"

"We are establishing a new company to rival Proteus. We can explain and show in detail how Proteus is intentionally trying to influence evangelicals and eliminate their distinctive beliefs. We are on a mission to counter this. We are calling our new company Abdiel."

"I'm on board," Emily said with a smile.

NOTES TO CHAPTERS

Chapter 12

1. Robert Peterson, *Hell on Trial: The Case for Eternal Punishment* (Phillipsburg: Presbyterian and Reformed Publishing Company, 1995), p. 110

2. Kathryn Gin Lum, *Damned Nation: Hell in America from the Revolution to Reconstruction* (New York: Oxford University Press, 2014), p. 117

Chapter 13

1. "Of the Morals of the Catholic Church," Augustine, Accessed March 31, 2018. http://www.newadvent.org/fathers/1401.htm

2. "AKA I've Got the Blues," *Jessica Jones,* Season 1 Scripts, Accessed March 31, 2018. https://genius.com/Jessica-Jones-aka-ive-got-the-blues-annotated

3. Alister McGrath, *Explaining Your Faith* (Baker Publishing Group, 1996)

4. John Calvin, *Institutes of Christian Religion* (Philadelphia: The Westminster Press, 1960), p. 35

5. Sinclair Ferguson, *The Christian Life: A Doctrinal Introduction* (Edinburgh: Banner of Truth Trust, 1981), p. 43

6. Thomas Ananias, *Summa Theologica*, Accessed April 10, 2018. http://www.newadvent.org/summa/1002.htm

7. John Milton, *Paradise Lost,* (New York: W. W. Norton & Company, 2005), p. 129

Chapter 16

1. Elizabeth Gerhardt, *The Cross and Gendercide: A Theological Response to Global Violence Against Women and Girls* (Downers Grove: IVP Academic, 2014), p. 13

2. Ibid, p. 14

ACKNOWLEDGEMENTS

I would like to dedicate this book to my wife Mignon.

A special thanks Mila for her work on the cover design. She captured what I was looking for in the cover. Contact Mila through her website at https://www.milagraphicartist.com/.

A thank you to Arnetta Jackson from Line Upon Line proofreading and transcription services for her help in proofreading and formatting the novel. Contact Arnetta through her website at https://www.lineuponlineservices.com/

Thank you to everyone who took time to read the book. A follow-up novel called *Proteus* is in the planning stages. For comments on it or on this novel, contact me at the following itcouldhappenhere9@gmail.com